BREACH

Book Two of the Dark Walker Series
By Shelly Campbell

EERIE RIVER PUBLISHING

To anyone who's ever felt alone and invisible. You matter.

Chapter One

Something worms up my nose, tickles my throat, and wriggles deep into my chest. I retch. A wet filament snakes up my cheek and into my nostril. At my touch, it twitches like a worm skewered by a fishhook. I yank it out and it rakes my throat all the way up. Gagging, I sit up, and focus through watering eyes. *This isn't the summer cottage.*

My mind is numb and detached. *And that's not a plastic tube.* I had one shoved up my nose in a children's hospital once when I got sick enough that I couldn't eat, and I've never forgotten the burn of it coming out or the rash from the tape on my cheek. What I'm grasping is different. It's an uneven diameter and covered in mucous. Looks like a tree root crossed with a tape worm. As I hold it at arm's length, long feathery antennae—*tentacles?*—stretch toward my face like a hairy plant reaching for the sun.

I yelp and hurl it against the wall. It sticks there like cooked spaghetti.

"Morning, Sunshine," a young woman's voice says. "I'd leave the ones in your leg alone if I were you."

That's when I feel the odd sensation below my knee, maggots fluttering beneath my skin. I tear off the blanket and reveal my bare legs. The left one is swollen, white and rubbery. And... *Oh God.* It's

anchored to the bed—not with straps. Delving deep into every laceration, are countless, bloated *root things*. They whip at my fingers as I pull them out of my wounds, impossibly long, slick with my blood, and scrabbling for purchase.

"Hey. Stop!" The girl says, but I don't.

The pain is unbelievable, but panic is stronger. As I rip out the squirming things one after another, an odd certainty grips me. *If I let go, they'll burrow as deep as they can go.* As soon as I've torn enough of them out to allow movement, I twist off the mattress and hit the floor hard, a wheezing mess of blood-flecked blankets and hiccupping cries.

Retreating, I bump into a warm body.

"Easy." A girl in a leather jacket grips my shoulder and I flinch at her touch. She's sitting on the floor beside her mattress. "Just breathe," she says.

My gaze stays pinned to the network of fibrous, bloody strands puddling beyond our feet, writhing, and balling up at their ends, thickening into a lumpy cable that disappears through a port in a plexiglass wall.

"What the fuck are those?" It hurts to talk. I don't know where I am. Who she is.

"You don't have IDOCS in your world?" she asks.

"Wha-what?" *My world.* My head reels, the pain in my leg echoes up my bones and whimpering sounds slip out of me. We're in a room. A round room, but I can't focus on anything except the terror tingling through my limbs.

"Intravenous dynamic organic capillary system. Thought everyone had them. They've been in hospitals here since the sixties."

"Uh ... no." I pull my knees up and wrap my bloody hands around them. I'm in a medical gown. Not crinkly paper. Something slick and synthetic. "Shit no."

"They've replaced IVs, scopes, and catheters," she continues nonchalantly.

"Catheters? Stop. Please." I wince. My hands are shaking. What happened to me?

"Would have given you a gentler heads up if I knew it was your first time with symbiotic medicine. Sorry, David."

That jolts me. *She knows my name. Did I tell her?* Wouldn't matter if I did. No-one remembers me. A memory tickles my mind: *"You wanna come out from under the couch, Sunshine? What's your name? Talk to me."*

And then it hits me: why my leg is cut all to hell, why my own family forgot me, the door, the skeleton key. Bizarro world beyond. How I'd fallen asleep at the lake and woken up after dark to a seething shoreline of maneaters swarming me. They'd come barreling after me into the cottage, tossing furniture—and pinning me under the overturned fold out couch—eager to swarm through the gateway into my world. But I'd broken the key off in the door and swallowed the half left behind. That had *really* pissed the maneaters off.

Then she'd charged in on an honest-to-God motorcycle, all blazing lights and hot exhaust, a four-stroke angel in scuffed steel-toed boots. She's still wearing those.

I stare at the worn-out toe caps to avoid looking at the wriggling abominations I just yanked out of me. "You saved me. Thank you."

She puts her hands behind her head and leans back against the mattress, a forced casualness. "You puked on my bike."

"I'm sorry." It doesn't sound convincing because I'm distracted by the jittering mess of tentacles retracting away from us, squeezing through the port in the wall until they're gone. A small door snicks closed over the hole in the curved plexiglass and the only hint that the creepy-as-hell things had ever existed is a Rorschach inkblot of blood on the floor and revulsion prickling my skin. What the hell is this place?

"You shouldn't have taken them out. You'd have healed faster." She blinks at the blood trickling down my shin. "The doctors'll be pissed. They'll want to put them back in."

Doctors. A hospital then? I take a deep breath through my nose. "Fuck. That. I'll chew my own leg off first."

She laughs. "That bad, huh?"

I steal a sidelong glance even though the small movement hurts. Everything hurts. *You got bitten by a venomous maneater, idiot. Of course, everything hurts. She knows why you're here. Maybe she can get you back home. Make eye contact. Just make conversation like a normal human being.* I can do that, right? Act like I'm used to being seen? Like when someone turns their full attention on me, I don't feel like a bug who's about to be stomped on? *Just pretend you're talking to James.* I clear my throat. "You're asking me like you've never used ... symbiotic medicine? You said it's been here forever."

She's got a great smile. She's wearing pearl stud earrings that don't match the rest of her practical get up. Her dark eyes meet mine and I fight against the overwhelming urge to look away.

"Never woke up with them still in, that's for damned sure," she says. "Busted a doctor's nose when they tried to integrate an IDOCS when I broke my wrist once. They thought I was 'adequately sedated', but gatekeeping messes with your metabolism and their dosing was way off. Doesn't look like they learned their lesson if you woke up with some of yours still installed."

"Gatekeeping?" I mumble. She'd said the word when she'd rescued me in Bizarro world. I'd never seen another human there before. More pieces click together through the fog in my mind. There'd been a bridge between my dimension and its hellscape mirror plane. I'd opened it when I found the key to the addition in the summer cottage. The maneaters had already razed everyone on that side and they were hungry for new blood. *My fault.* I'd opened the door. Put my own family in their line of fire. My whole world.

"The door's closed?" My voice cracks. "I broke it, right?" I *need* to know that my family is safe, James and Dad. Mom and the twins.

All of them. I need to be 100% sure that I fixed the awful danger I'd unwittingly put them all in.

"You did," she answers.

Relief floods me and I sag against the shock of it. I'd barely broken the bridge in time. I'd thrown my life away to save my family and everyone else in a world that had tried to erase me for as long as I can remember. That should make me feel *something,* shouldn't it?

It doesn't.

I mean, it's pretty hard to contemplate lofty self sacrifices when you're still coming down from evicting a pile of parasitic whip worms from their comfy domicile down your throat and inside your leg. She'd said I woke up with *some* of mine still in. Meaning there'd been more of the things in me at some point. *Please not a catheter.* I shudder and glance around the odd pod-shaped room containing us.

Two bunks flank a miniscule, enclosed toilet/shower combo. Other than my blood track, the white, seamless acrylic floor is spotless, and it's glowing. A ring of recessed lighting circles its outer edge. We're surrounded by a plexiglass globe, riddled with air vents and small access ports. There's a 360-degree camera mounted directly overhead. I can't see a door big enough to fit a person through.

It's dark outside our bubble ... and dirty. Threadbare tarps slung over slack ropes wall us in. A few bulky cables snake across the floor, presumably powering our pod. Open web steel joists arc far overhead, streaked white with bird shit. Muddy clusters of communal swallows' nests sprout like cancerous growths clinging to the rafters and moonlight oozes through a cobwebbed skylight. This is no hospital. A warehouse maybe?

"Where are we?" I croak. Numbness curls off me like an orange peel. Beneath it, I'm all soft, fleshy fear and jittery pain.

She spreads her arms wide. "Welcome to the hamster ball."

The ache in my leg feels like someone swapped out my bone marrow for glowing coals. I remember riding bitch on her motorcycle, repelling the maneaters with unnaturally bright banks of light, but I can't scrape together the rest of the trip. "Is this…" my voice wobbles so badly that I stop, lick my lips, and try again. "Is this a jail?"

She tightens the knot on the bandana holding back her halo of tight curls. "You been in jail before, Sunshine?"

Yeah, plenty of times. Tagging along with my dad to fetch Jord and Jess out of the drunk tank. Never on this side of the partition though. *I miss them. God, I even miss my idiot twin brothers.* Get your head on straight or you're never getting back to them. "No jail. I'm a real boy scout," I say.

Confusion flits across her face. I don't think she knows what a boy scout is. "Well, we don't have jails here. We're in quarantine. Job hazard. You'll get used to it."

Where's here? I frown down at my hospital gown. She's not wearing one. Only me. "We're sick?" I don't feel sick, do I? Tired? Yes. Sore, battered, and bleeding? Sure. Freaked out? Hell to the yeah. But I don't feel *ill.*

"Probably not, but it's Embassy standard procedure. Any time I rescue a stray puppy from another world, they want to make sure it doesn't have rabies."

Oh good. She likes me. I'm a rabid puppy. *Way to go, David.* Her words are obviously intended to sting, but I'm too tired to rise to the bait. I want to keep her talking. I need a voice. An anchor. Any voice. My heartbeat rattles faster in my head every time this freaking room falls into silence. *Another world?* She said we're in another world. I can't handle thinking about that right now. So, I swallow and revert to the only defense I have left, ill-timed humour. "I promise I won't piss on the floor if you scratch behind my ear."

She snort-laughs. "No dice. Last guy said the same thing and he pissed everywhere." There's an odd undertone to her voice. Cagey.

So, I'm not the first 'puppy' she's rescued. This isn't the first time she's been stuck in here because some higher-up is worried she brought back a disease from another world—and I'm gathering from the scuffs and gouges on the plexiglass walls that not all of her other roommates were pleasant during their stay. That explains the cold shoulder. She's been quarantined with assholes before. A woman stuck alone in here with strangers, some of them guys who were likely stronger than she was. Of course, she'd be on guard. If I want her to help me, then she has to think I'm harmless. Shouldn't be a hard sell. I am. I can't even look her in the eye without breaking into a sweat.

"I'm sorry I barfed on your bike," I say. "And I'm sorry you're stuck in here because of me. I'm just—This..." I circle a finger over my head and break eye contact. "This is all a bit much. I didn't even get your name."

She leans over and offers her palm. Our shoulders touch when she does, and I'm suddenly overly aware of the fact that I'm sitting bare-assed on the floor in an open-backed gown next to a pretty girl. Her nails are clipped short. Small, raised scars criss-cross the dark brown skin on the back of her hand.

"Charlie," she says.

I wipe my fingers down the front of my gown and shake my head. I'm not used to this. Being someone's sole focus. It feels like ants crawling down my neck. "I-I don't want to get blood on you. Nice to meet you, Charlie."

She doesn't budge. "So, you'll puke on my bike, but you won't shake my hand. You scared of girls?"

"Terrified, yeah." I clean my hand the best I can and grip hers briefly. "I'm David."

"You told me already." She breaks into a smile.

I'm so used to people forgetting me and having to repeat my name. Start with something simple. Get your bearings. "Charlie, can you tell me why I'm dressed for the occasion and you're not?"

She points to my bed and then back to hers. I notice for the first time that mine has a bank of analytical equipment clipped to the outside wall. Coiled up IDOCS are plugged into them. There's no suite of screens next to Charlie's bed. "You're the guinea pig. Or hamster, I guess. You're the one they're interested in."

My leg feels like it's on fire now. The IDOCS must have been pumping me up with painkillers before I tore them out. My ears are ringing, filling my head with the hungry sound of mosquitoes. I can barely focus on what she's saying. "Who's they, exactly?"

"The Embassy. They thought they lost you eons ago. It happens. Lots of kids never come back from their safe house worlds. Lots of parents never documented where they sent them well enough. Everything is messy like that in war. They lost track, or died, or couldn't get back their kids if a gate broke—"

"Wait. War?"

Charlie frowns at my interruption and smooths her cloud of hair back. "Yeah. I don't know if you noticed, but there's a massive alien invasion going on. And we're trying to stop it."

Maneaters. I blink down at the ugly wound on my leg.

"No-one's ever lived away from Prime as long as you have. Not all in one stint. Some of us have survived four or five years in a foster dimension, but … how old are you?"

This is too much. All this talking. All this information metastasizing in my head, pressing against my brain like swelling tumors. War. Safe worlds. Prime. Where's Prime?

"David?" Charlie says.

"What?" I blink at her. My heart is crashing in my chest, and I can't stop my hands from shaking.

"How old are you?"

"Uh, s-seventeen."

"Shit. *Seventeen years?* That's unheard of. You're a variant the docs have never seen before. They like to pick those apart and see what makes them tick."

Shit no. I've got to get out of here. I've got to make sure my family is okay, and that James's ankle is healing. The maneaters reached under the door and tried to pull him under long before they latched onto me. What if his infection is worse than mine and technology back home isn't good enough to fix it? Fear must be written all over my face because Charlie bumps her shoulder into mine again and softens her voice, "Don't worry. The Embassy just wants DNA samples, blood tests, and a billion boring interviews before they reintegrate you into society."

"*Re*-integrate?" My head is spinning. I think I'm going to puke or pass out.

"Welcome home, Sunshine. It's been a hot minute."

Home. What? Oh ... Holy shit. I'm from here? The wrong side? I've always felt it, but coming from someone else, the confirmation feels like a baseball bat to the head.

I barely make it to the tiny bathroom before I throw up. I don't have enough time to close the janky accordion door and, if you're wearing a hospital gown, it's impossible to vomit into a toilet without your ass hanging out, so Charlie sees *everything*.

Fantastic. Just fantastic.

Chapter Two

There's plenty of time to catch up on history lessons. Charlie says that quarantine lasts for fourteen days, no exceptions, and I was only out of it for one. Lots of opportunities to make an ass out of myself in front of the girl who saved my life. Lucky.

What I know so far: I'm in an observation pod—a *Hamster Ball*—in a world called Prime. It's not Bizarro world. It's a dozen dimensions below that and—supposedly—it's my home. I don't know if I fully believe that. Nothing homey about this place. It's all sterilized anonymity, cold, analytical machinery, and dusty abandonment.

Except for her.

Once you get past the snappiness, my roomie is patient and considerate. That first day, after I was sick, she propped me up in the shower, undid the ties on the back of my gown and turned her head away when I handed it out to her. I stayed in there with my forehead pressed against the stainless steel and hot water sluicing down my back until my leg wouldn't let me stand anymore. I do my best crying in the shower, but I didn't have the energy for a cathartic ugly sob, and I didn't know what the hell to do next. I was puffy-eyed and naked, but Charlie tapped on the accordion door to let me know there was a towel and a stack of folded clothes waiting for me. There were also several rolls of bandages and a silver tube of gel that smelled like disinfectant. I had no idea where it came from or who brought it, but footprints scuffed the dirty floor outside our pod. She bandaged my leg, and I slept after that, utterly overwhelmed. Useless as a damned puppy.

I've met my captors since then. Everyone comes dressed in puffy white hazmat suits, plodding past the fraying tarped dividers like astronauts. The doctors carry tongue swabs, needles, and capped test tubes. When they need to, they come into the pod via the main entry. It takes two separate keys to activate it, like a nuclear warhead. The whole Plexiglas bubble rotates upward, and a big port scrolls out of the floor. That's why Charlie calls it a hamster ball 'cause it rolls on its horizontal axis.

The Embassy men carry guns and notebooks. They look like secret service guys in the movies, like they drink propaganda for breakfast, and break people like me before lunch. They never come into the pod, just set up folding chairs outside, and ask me endless questions through the intercom system. They're the only face of the Embassy I've seen, and this is the fourth time they've been here in two days. It's debilitatingly exhausting. All this attention. Their gazes peeling me down layer by layer. All. The. Talking. Jesus.

"You said you felt more at home in the dimensions that bridged to your safe world?" A man with hard blue eyes and a thin navy tie holds his pen poised over his notebook.

Dimensions. *Plural.* I've been informed that what I fondly referred to as Bizarro world wasn't just one place, but hundreds of different dimensions. Each time I opened the door to a different time, I opened it to a different branch too. See, every time I feel like I'm processing something about this place, they casually toss me another mind-blowing fact and expect me to digest it without melting down or going numb. *Answer them. They're trying to figure out what happened just like you are.* I try to convince myself that they're not my enemy just

because I'm trapped in a small space, and they're on the other side of the glass, but that's a hard pill to swallow. "Yeah, I felt better on the wrong side," I say.

"Did you notice time passing differently in the dimensions you bridged to?"

"It stood still on my side."

He fires a quick glance at his partner before saying, "Clarify?"

"I could spend all day on the maneater side and when I got back, maybe ten seconds passed on my side. If I went over for less than half an hour, no time passed at all."

"More time must have passed." The guy with the gun snorts and I'm instantly ticked-off at his tone.

"I looked at the clock before I went in and when I came out. I know what I saw."

The interviewer scrubs his forehead. "You're certain the timepiece you referenced was operable and you were reading it correctly?"

Are they legit asking me if I can tell time? "It was ticking, and I can read a clock."

"Why did you break your ticket and eat it?" They've asked me this question every time they've visited. It feels like an interrogation. Like they suspect some sort of malicious logic behind my actions. Like I hadn't just been shitting my pants trying to keep the Pithos key away from the aliens that wanted to leap onto my side and devour my family and everyone else. "I told you. I don't know. I just didn't want the maneaters to get a hold of it, I guess."

The one with the gun shakes his head and snorts. "They'd have scooped you open like a melon if they wanted it."

"Thanks for the visual." I suppress a shudder. So, the only thing that saved me from a swift evisceration is that broken tickets don't work. As soon as the Pithos key snapped in half, the maneaters lost interest in it. Put that away for your broken brain to chew on later.

"Have you ever previously ingested broken tickets?" The thin tie guy asks.

Christ, why are they so hyper-focused on me swallowing stuff? "No. I didn't even know what a ticket was before Charlie told me."

"So, you're telling us you marooned yourself in an infected dimension expecting to die in order to break the bridge to your safe world, is that correct?"

"Yes."

"And before this particular instance, you never collapsed a bridge by breaking a ticket and eating the remnants?"

"No, no other bridges. Look, I don't know who you guys think I am. I haven't even graduated from high school."

He changes tack and starts probing about my childhood.

"Any major illnesses, diseases or conditions during infancy?"

"I don't remember infancy," I snap.

Tie Guy emits a sigh that slumps his big shoulders. His partner's hand twitches on his gun.

Note. Don't be snarky to the armed stiff. I can't help it. How is it possible to feel cornered in a circular room? Why do they have to keep staring the whole time?

"Did your caretakers inform you of any illnesses, diseases or conditions during infancy?"

"My caretakers? You mean my parents?" I swallow at the ache that rises in my throat when I think of them. My family, who I have no conclusive evidence that I saved. James looked awful on that last day. *What if he already died from that leg infection? What if he's dying right now, and medicine here could save him?* The awful thoughts stab at me and I swallow hard.

"Any illnesses during infancy?" Tie Guy repeats.

"I, uh, I had all the regular stuff. Chicken pox. Measles maybe? I was small for my age. I guess I had digestion problems and had to get a feeding tube a few times."

"Failure to thrive," the gunman interjects and Tie Guy jots something in his book.

"Any long-term conditions or medications?" he says.

"I get migraines." None since I got here. Nothing but the occasional ringing in my ears now. Charlie says I feel better because I'm back home. She says I felt like I belonged in Bizarro worlds because they were closer to Prime than the world I grew up in. I don't know if I believe her—if I believe I'm from Prime. It feels too much like the plot of a cheesy comic book. I'd remember if this place was home, wouldn't I? I'd sense it. And I'd feel better than this. More put together. By rights, I'm supposed to be feeling superhuman, but maneater venom is one hell of a kryptonite. Charlie told me that too.

"Migraines? On a prescription?"

"Yeah. Imitrex."

"That a brand name?"

"Yes."

"Do you know the medication's generic name?"

"Uh, Sumatriptan, I think."

"Selective serotonin receptor?"

"Sure." How the hell am I supposed to know? Why won't they just leave?

"Any chest pain or arrythmia while you were medicated?"

"No."

"Stomach or intestinal bleeding? You said you had digestive issues."

"When I was little. I didn't go on meds for the headaches until I was older."

"What age?"

"I don't know. Ten or eleven maybe?"

"Allergies?"

"None."

"Recreational drugs?"

"Yes please."

"Just answer the question Mr. Enril," the gunman says.

"What did you call me?" I frown, scratching my arms.

They ignore me. "Do you or have you used recreational drugs?" Thin Tie asks.

"Cigarettes or harder stuff?"

"Any of it."

"I have the odd can of beer and I smoke. Hey, who's Mr. Enril?" *'Cause he sounds like a serial killer.*

"Can you think of a time when your caretakers and their children contracted an illness, and you did not?"

"Nope." I can't tamp my temper down for much longer. Every time he calls my parents *caretakers* like they're nothing more than school janitors, I want to deck him, but I bite it back because I'm scared that I'll never get out of this pod if I don't play nice. Never be able to see my family again or protect them against these worlds I tied them to.

"Have you ever been ill and no-one else in your caretaker's family contracted it?"

"Nothing serious. Stomach flu maybe? Migraines."

"Have you ever experienced unexplained seizures?"

"No."

"Any urinary tract infections recently?"

"No." Oh, Jesus. They *did* put in a catheter when I was out. I don't want to think about that.

"Have you ever been diagnosed with or tested positive for a sexually transmitted disease?"

Seriously? "No."

"Are you currently sexually active?"

My cheeks burn. I glance at Charlie. "Like right now? Gross. There's an overhead camera. You guys into that kinky shit?"

"How many sexual partners have you had in the last year?"

"Do I have to answer this?" I squirm.

"You do."

"Zero." *Let's get off the topic of David's non-existent sex life now, shall we?*

Charlie is studying me. I can see it out of the corner of my eye. It's one more invisible spider on my skin.

"How many sexual partners have you had previous to the last year?"

Jesus, they're taking no prisoners. I scrub my chin. "Like ever?"

"Correct."

"Zero," I sigh.

It goes on like this forever, an eternal application for medical insurance with the universe's most pedantic provider. Every day these Embassy stiffs have more inane questions, and they won't answer any of mine. *I just want to be alone. I just want to check that my family is okay, is that too damned much to ask?*

When they finally leave, Charlie stretches and says, "Zeeeeroooo."

"Shut up." I flop back onto my bed and drape my arm over my face, wrung out, skin prickling with frustration. The interrogators rankling voices are knotting together in my head, scraping at the inside of my skull like something trapped and frantic. "How in the hell was that a relevant question?" I blurt.

"They wanna know if you've seeded your safe world full of Prime super babies."

"Gross."

"You're not half bad looking, Sunshine. Why zero? Asexual?"

I'm about the furthest thing from asexual there is. Okay, maybe not the furthest thing. I'm not some sort of raging sex addict or any-thing because how can you even be addicted to something you've never had ... with a partner? "I'm awkward as hell. I've got acne, and—until recently—I've been coasting along, invisible to everyone in my world. The opportunity hasn't come up, alright?"

"Sorry," she says. And she doesn't press it. You don't needle people you're stuck in a hamster ball with for two weeks.

I say my next words quietly because they terrify me. "That was my last name, wasn't it? Enril. They slipped up and said it. They've ID'd me, haven't they?" And if they have, that means they found me on a list somewhere. In an archive. That means I'm actually from here. It makes all this unavoidably real.

Charlie blinks up at the transparent ceiling of our globe, eyes unfocusing, gaze pinned to the dirty skylight far above. It's the only indication of day and night we have and it's getting dark out. As she cranes her neck, I notice she has a tattoo, a flock of origami cranes that curve from behind her left ear and follow the hollow of her neck down to her collarbone. "They've taken your fingerprints and bodily fluids enough times by now to compare your DNA to the records in the missing children database."

"So, they know who my..." The idea of what I'm about to say feels so foreign and wrong it sticks in my throat. "Who my biological family is?"

She purses her lips. "Lots of families haven't survived the war, David. The Embassy would tell you if your family was still alive."

My ears are ringing. I shake my head. It's overwhelming me again, the impossibility of all this, the incongruity, the interviews, the being utterly 100%, twenty-four hours a day *visible* in a confined space with another human being who I don't know. It feels like standing naked in front of an audience while someone's trying to hypnotize me. My chest tightens and my breathing comes too fast, too loud. "Do you think we can get them to shut off the lights for a bit?"

"Sorry, it's all automated."

The electric whine of the machinery outside the wall next to my bed sounds like a dentist's drill, exposing raw nerves and tensing every muscle in my body. I can't do this anymore. I want to go home, which is an exceedingly weird feeling since every day I spend here is confirming it wasn't *home*. I want to hug my dad and hear James's voice. I want to curl up somewhere dark and quiet and hibernate. I want the Goddamned noise to stop. If Charlie asks me one more question on top of all the others, I'll snap. I'll probably dissolve into tears like a tired toddler—which is not, I believe, recommended anywhere in *How to Win Friends and Influence People.*

Instead, I pull my blanket over my head and say, "Run me through it one more time. From the beginning?" I need to know how this world works so I don't make mistakes again, so I can build as many walls as possible between my family and the maneaters, even if it means walling them off from me. My *real* family. Not the Enrils—whoever the hell they are.

She lets out a long sigh. "Again?"

"Please. I just want... I can't..."

We've gone through this countless times in our hours of downtime. Over the past two days, she's patiently answered questions and coached my breathing when we got to the hard parts, but no matter how many times I hear it, none of it seems real. How can it? We're trapped in a damned bubble.

She must sense how close I am to the end of my rope because, bless her, she starts into the history of Prime without any annoyance bleeding into her voice. "Our universe is like a tree. Prime's the central trunk—our scientist's think so, anyways."

Prime is a lower dimension from the one Charlie rescued me from. There are no maneaters here yet.

"At some point, our ancestors figured out they could travel to nearby *twigs.*"

"Like parallel worlds?" I swallow, staring at the weave of the blanket. "I step on a butterfly and the world splits?"

"Not quite. Worlds don't split *every* time something changes, it's unpredictable. Quantum physics is a real bitch."

That should be on a t-shirt.

Charlie continues. "We haven't pinned down the criteria for branching yet. There are boughs of Prime that split off—a few thousand different versions of our world. The original gatekeepers figured out how to jump between them. They manifested the first bridges."

She sighs. "And then they went on some road trips. Pretty random at first. Cautious. Exploratory. Just dipping their toes. But the government directed the later expeditions, extracting resources, adopting future tech, cheating death, changing history.

"The process for building bridges leaked. A black market for tickets cropped up. Soon anyone could be a gatekeeper and travel anywhere. It went to shit pretty quick after that. We went too fast. Corporations all racing to plant their flags first. Everyone ignoring the field experts asking us to slow down and gauge the possible consequences of our actions." She shrugged. "We tangled everything up. Lost track of how many bridges we built and where all the tickets ended up."

"Tickets. Like my key."

"Some tickets are keys, yeah," Charlie continues. "They can be anything really, so long as they puzzle into some sort of bridge." Her nose scrunches as she ticks off examples on her fingers. "Door card and swipe lock entry. Toll coin and booth. That sort of thing. I've even seen an arrowhead that opened a bridge in a cave made of the stone it was knapped from. Original keepers did their best to make their tickets out of something that would last and match up to plenty of bridges. Lots of redundancy in case something in the system failed."

I frown. "My bridge collapsed on its own. The first few times I tried to go in, it was … patchy. Sometimes there wasn't another world behind the door, just a regular room."

"That's a safety too. The bridges were engineered to fail if they haven't been used for a time. If a ticketholder doesn't cross for awhile, the connection dissolves so the two worlds don't stay snarled together. That was the idea anyways. Doesn't look like the ancients knew about keystones at the start. They learned it the hard way, I guess."

She sounds so desolate that I flip the blanket down and turn to face her. My eyes hurt. *Goddamnit, would it kill them to turn down the lights?* "Keystones. Those are things left on the wrong side, right? They lock the bridge in place." Everett, the guy who'd stayed in the cottage before us, he'd accidentally left his tobacco tin in one of the Bizarro worlds. Later, the maneaters had snagged the strawberry print dish towel under the door from my side and ate it. Both times, it made the bridge to Bizarro world impossible to close.

Charlie breaks eye contact. She tugs on one of her pearl earrings. "Yeah. Things." For a long time, she doesn't say anything else, just sits there staring at her boots, nostrils flared, chapped lips pinched, her breathing as even as a metronome.

I'm crap at reading people, but even I can tell when someone's holding back. "How old were you when your parents sent you away, Charlie?"

We've gone over this already. How maneaters scouted into worlds, but then they had rapidly turned into massive, choking mobs in the millions. Ravenous. Unstoppable. They devoured entire populations in days. The gatekeepers couldn't untangle all the dimensions fast enough to contain the alien spread. There were just too many breaches. Didn't help that some keepers refused to collapse bridges.

In the face of annihilation, a cult faction sprung up, vocally insisting that the dimensions they'd woven together were *meant* to be intertwined. Basically, Prime couldn't stop the stampede it started, and families who could afford it sent their children off world to shelter in "safe worlds", foster dimensions that hadn't yet been breached. A last-ditch effort to shield the next generation from the war that looked to be coming home to their parents. It was supposed to be temporary.

It was. For most kids. Just my luck that I'd be a forgotten child in this world too.

"When did my parents send me away? Near as I can figure, I was a year old. They, uh…" Charlie turns from me and clears her throat. "They dropped me in a hospital. I guess it took a couple of days until I was visible enough for anyone to notice me."

"How long were you there?"

"Three years. I was really sick by the time they brought me back."

Something's off. I can't let go of it even though Charlie's expression is hardening into stone. I try to picture her wandering the aseptic halls of a hospital, tiny, crying, and unseen. "How could you remember that? You were a toddler when you left, and four when you got back. Little kids don't remember shit like that."

Her lips twitch. She glances at the camera overhead, and my breath snarls up in my chest. "Maybe I've got a photographic memory," she says flatly.

Bullshit. She's lying. She's gone back, I realize. Charlie's revisited the world she fostered in, probably more than once if she remembers it so well. And that worried look toward the camera, *that* was because she doesn't want the Embassy goons with guns to know about those visits. Makes sense. She'd told me yesterday that once children were deposited into their safe worlds, the bridges were broken, and no parental contact was allowed.

Unbreached dimensions were a rarity, and they only remained safe so long as their gateways remained closed. Cutting off all contact was the only way to protect the children who were sent away from maneater invasions. Maybe Charlie's been breaking the law and I just narced her out. Maybe she could help me check in on my family.

That last thought drives nostalgic pain so deep into my chest, I can barely breathe past it.

I should shut up before I dig this hole deeper, but I can't. A troubling thought grips me and it won't let go. Charlie's glaring daggers at me, all smudged mascara, torn denim, and iron spine. The softness in her is gone, but the question bursts out of me anyways. "How did they break the bridges to the safe worlds?"

"What?" Her nose wrinkles.

I sit straighter, gripping the edge of the bed with both hands. "How did Prime stick children into safe worlds and collapse the bridges behind them? You said that keystones are objects left on the wrong side that hold the door open. People are too. I was doing it, wasn't I?

holding the bridge to my safe world open even after the dish towel rotted away in a maneater's belly because *I* was still on the wrong side." Everett was too. Suddenly I can't get enough air.

Everett had killed himself to break the bridge because the keystone he'd lost wouldn't biodegrade like mine did. And he couldn't think of any other way to close what he'd opened. I'd been attempting to do the same when Charlie found me. At the end of my rope. Trying to fix my mistakes and blow up a bridge to protect a family that wouldn't even remember me. *Oh shit. Oh Jesus, please let me be wrong.* I curl over my knees and take deep, trembling breaths through my nose.

"I think we're done talking about this for today," Charlie says quietly.

"The *fuck* we are," I bark. It echoes off the plexiglass walls and her boots squeak as she recoils. I stand up, feeling drunk and sick and dizzy. "All us kids. How did we get planted in other worlds without becoming keystones? How did they close the doors behind us if we were all on the wrong side?"

She stands braced with one hand tucked behind her back, under her jacket. With a start, I realize she's probably armed. Makes sense. The Embassy wouldn't leave a gatekeeper defenseless in quarantine with someone from another world who was likely to be freaked out, or violent.

And I'm freaking out.

Charlie's voice is as flat and cold as the air wheezing through the filtering system. "The Embassy thought there were only two ways to break a bridge before we met you, Sunshine." She holds up a finger. "Keep everything on its own side. With no keystones in place, if you don't use a bridge, it self-closes. But, if you've got cross-contamination—anything other than a ticket in a world it doesn't belong in? You're screwed unless you get everything back in its proper place or your keystone biodegrades like yours did. But the thing is, even then, you didn't actually put *everything* back in its proper place, did you, David?"

"What?" I frown.

"*You* were still cross-contamination, you understand? A live keystone. After you left your safe world, you were still on the wrong side because you weren't from your foster world or the infested ones. Your proper place is here. Prime." She motions around us. "Your bridge shouldn't have burned while you were still alive. It goes against every prevailing theory. That's the big news flash, why the Embassy is so damned interested in you. You just showed us that if you break your ticket and then eat it, like you did, you can collapse a bridge even if there's a live keystone holding it open. And you can survive it." She fades off again. "This war is about burning bridges, stemming the flow of invaders, limiting fatalities and you just showed the Embassy a new way to do all that. They'll want to replicate that, David."

She's trying to steer the conversation away from my question. "What's the last way?" I ask.

"What?"

"To break a bridge?" Her jaw twitches so I repeat myself. "What was the last way, Charlie? You said you knew two ways before you met me." I think I know what it is. I think I'm going to be sick.

She purses her lips and pins me with a wary stare before speaking slowly. "Kill the gatekeeper who opened the bridge. A bridge breaks if its ticketholder dies."

Like Everett. I wipe my mouth with a shaking hand and meet Charlie's hard gaze even though it physically hurts to do so. I need to make 100% sure I'm not misunderstanding her. "There were no open bridges left into our safe worlds, right?"

"No open bridges," she confirms quietly.

"So, who ... who did they..." I can't finish. For several seconds all I can do is swallow the taste of bile and wait for her to put me out of my misery.

"I told you we don't have jails," she says. "We've got plenty of criminals though. The most serious crimes will earn you a death sentence as a keystone mule."

"I don't know what that is."

"When the Embassy was dispatching emergency teams abroad, they made a discovery about group travel. Whoever is holding the ticket when the bridge is first crossed, they're the *primitus* keystone." She pauses, notes my confusion, and explains. "The main keystone. It doesn't matter how much cargo you move between worlds, if you kill the primitus—the ticketholder—the bridge collapses no matter what or who is on the wrong side. Keystone mules are criminals the Embassy wants to get rid of, but they use them as a tool first. With mules, they can move whatever they like between dimensions without worrying about leaving a mess of bridges behind."

I swallow hard. "Why wouldn't a person, a m-mule, not just make a break for it in the dimension they're sent to? If they're going to be executed anyway, why not just run?"

"Some do. It's a bad end, that. They're sent with an armed escort who's been instructed to give them a slow death if they try to escape and a quick, painless one if they behave. Rich parents *bought* keystone mules from the Embassy. They paid through the teeth to get tickets and armed escorts to transport their children to safe worlds away from the invasions, and most insisted on having the mules brought back home so they could witness the primitus executions afterward. They wanted proof that the bridges were closed and their children secure."

My throat aches but I speak through the thickness. "Jesus Christ. What did parents with no money do?"

"They didn't send their kids away." Charlie breaks eye contact and picks at her lip. Her breathing slows down again, and I recognize it as a defense mechanism. She goes into zen mode when she wants to disappear.

"Or?" I press, and then I feel like shit because she looks back up with tears in her brown eyes.

"Or one of them volunteered to be a primitus themselves, and killed themselves as soon as they knew their kid was safe."

"Oh my God. Shit. Charlie," I say. "Your parents?"

She nods.

"I'm sorry. I'm…"

She presses a hand under her nose and turns away.

I want to say more, but I suck at this, comforting people, conversation in general. My mind feels jagged and full of holes. I lie back down, numb with realization. Mr. and Mrs. Enril. *If I'm actually from here. If those are my biological parents. They're either murderers or martyrs.*

Chapter Three

DAY… I DON'T KNOW. MORE THAN 16.

"They're neverrr gonna lemmeeoutta here." My throat feels like I swallowed sandpaper. It takes all my energy to push the garbled words out. I've been sedated and IDOCS have been reinserted in my leg. They're twitching and prickly under my skin, like microscopic millipedes, flocking to the most infected areas of my wound. I want to scream. I want to peel my skin off and claw the wretched things out, but my arms and legs are strapped to the bed to prevent it. Things have gotten … worse. Definitely worse.

I was supposed to be feeling better than I ever had in my life. That's what the doctors had insinuated. Prime was my supposed home world, and all the other retrieved children had enjoyed vastly improved health once they'd been brought back. I did too, at first. For a whole week, I felt lighter and stronger. The Embassy lackeys had given Charlie and me a pile of old paperbacks and board games so we wouldn't climb the walls in our boredom. In a strange way, it had reminded me of rainy days at the cottage when my whole family was trapped inside and entertaining themselves as best they could. It hurt to think of them. But I was working toward a plan to check on them and help James if he needed it. Charlie was my ticket. If she'd gone back to her safe world behind the Embassy's back, she'd know how to get me to mine.

Every morning, I woke up and my head didn't hurt. My shoulders didn't ache. I felt like I'd had the best sleep of my life, and someone had taken the liberty of giving me a full body massage while I was out. Charlie and I had been stuck in close confines for two weeks and I was getting more comfortable talking with her, but we weren't *that* close. Jesus, she'd slit my throat if she knew I was even thinking about her massaging me.

Anyways, I felt superhuman for about a week and then my health just nose dived. I started getting dizzy spells. The ringing in my ears got louder. The infection in my leg flared and I couldn't keep food down. It's been steadily downhill since then.

"Of course, they're going to let you out. You're getting better." Charlie sits on the floor beside my bed and holds my hand. She's done it the last two times I've had IDOCS sessions. Normally, I'd recoil from physical contact like this, but it's different with her now. It's comforting, like it's supposed to be. I want to thank her, but everything I say sounds like I'm sloppy drunk. She has calloused fingers. I don't think I've ever held a girl's hand. I mean, maybe in pre-school when we had to buddy up with someone and hang onto a rope on field trips. I'm damned sure I clung to somebody after the first bunch of times I got left behind. And that's what Charlie's doing now, letting me cling to her because I'm hopelessly lost. The tranquilizers are really messing with me. It's not like normal sleep. It's darker, more viscous. Pulling myself out of it feels like swimming far from shore, limbs too rubbery and stiff with cold to keep myself afloat, that shocking first accidental breath of briny water. I usually come to screaming. I doubt that's what Charlie expected to deal with in quarantine, but here we are.

You're a pretty stand-up roomie, I want to say, but what comes out is "You're ... pretty."

"Thanks." She doesn't look up, just keeps frowning at the magazine in her lap. "All the delusional guys think so."

"I'm not." I try to turn my head. It's hard to focus. *Oh God, if this is what maneater venom does, if James is declining like this, I'm running out of time to save him.*

"Not delusional?" She turns a page and studies a photo of a green motorcycle with its rider leaning into a turn so hard, their padded knee is grazing the blurred asphalt track. "You seem pretty loopy to me."

"No not..." I shudder as one of the IDOCS hits a nerve deep in my leg, close to my shin bone. I'm pumped up on painkillers, but I can still feel the sensation of the ghastly thing, poking around inside me. It's wrong to feel something alive that far within me. "Notgettinbetter. They'll keeepmehere, poke me fullaholes forever." I sniff loudly. I want to wipe my nose, but I can't reach it. My heartbeat pulls at my throat fast and urgent, like a rabbit clawing behind my ribs and I take deep thready breaths because I know the IDOCS will sedate me fully if I get panicky and God. Fuck. I can't. I'm scared of the gravity of that sleep. It's hungry. Like the maneaters behind the door were. It's a darkness that's tasted me before and now it wants to suck the meat from my bones. I don't know if I'm strong enough to swim away from it right now. I can't move. I can't MOVE. "Undothe sstraps, p-please," I gulp.

Charlie lets go of my hand. "They're not going to keep you here forever, David. And you've only got a half hour of treatment left."

I won't last that long. "Please." The word bleeds out of me. "I don-wannit...putme asleep." It's not just the darkness. The IDOCS installs extra tubes when it puts me under. There are holes I'd rather not have explored again, thanks very much.

She shifts to face me. Brown eyes so dark they look black, cloud of hair brushing my arm. "Promise you won't pull them out and I'll undo your arms."

"Yes." I nod and blink against the tears pooling in the corners of my eyes. "Promise." Gosh, I'm good at this. Impressing girls with my tough guy act. I should give motivational speeches. I should write a book.

Charlie stands and undoes my wrists, and I cover my face with both my hands and focus on taking deep, steady breaths. She smells like leather and citrus. I recognize the shampoo from the washroom cubicle. Apparently, the Embassy uses 'uplifting' scents because they help alleviate depression in subjects held in quarantine. Yes, we've talked about the shampoo in the bathroom. It's been a long stay and Charlie's really good at deflecting the conversation away from herself while simultaneously offering up interesting facts about virtually anything else.

"James. Whatifhee..." My mouth feels like I got teeth pulled and the freezing hasn't worn off yet. *Just speak. Say one damned thing that doesn't sound stupid.* I've told Charlie about my brother, how the maneaters tried to pull him under the locked door as he sleepwalked. She explained that the creatures can reach through gateways, like caged animals grabbing between the bars. They can fish for stuff like people and dish towels and tickets and pull them onto their side, but they can't get through themselves, not without a ticket. Why? Something about their physiology is too different. That's the best the Embassy can figure. I told her how James's leg had been mangled, same as mine and I can't stop thinking about it. "Whatif he'sssick like me?"

"He's not. This isn't dark walker venom. Those wounds are infection prone, yeah. But, not like this..." She trails off for so long that I let my hands drop from my face and stare at her. She moves away from my bed and starts pacing, avoiding my gaze. The Embassy has given her shit for slipping up and telling me about primitus keystones and mules. And her parents. I don't know when—sometime when I was out cold—but I can tell she's had her wrist slapped because she hasn't shared anything remotely personal since. Sometimes it feels like I'm talking to a help desk instead of Charlie.

Oh Shit. The thought plows into me. "You talktothadoctors withow me?"

"You've been sleeping a lot."

Not sleep. Something worse. "Is the key isenit?" I'd swallowed half of an alien artifact, one that was designed to rip holes through time and space and braid together entire dimensions. Everyone and their dog have been asking me questions about it, running me through mobile scanners searching for it. Hell, the Embassy's probably monitoring everything we flush down the toilet to see if I shit it out. They're hoping if they get their hands on it, they can replicate my neat little trick of breaking a keystone reinforced bridge without killing anyone. That'd be one hell of a boost to the war effort, especially with Prime's population as precarious as Charlie says it is. David, the bridge-breaker. The secret weapon. The gate crasher. Something about the broken key is special, or something about me.

"Yeah, the key." Charlie says. "They were hoping the IDOCS could extract it for you."

I shudder at that, the thought of the hungry things going further than eating up infected skin, stapling together torn muscle, or shunting out waste. The idea of them tunnelling deep through my guts to retrieve something I swallowed weeks before makes my breathing come so fast that something beeps on the machinery outside. The IDOCS dig deeper like they're bracing themselves, and a cold feeling slips through the veins in my leg. *Aw Shit. Shit. Shit. Stay awake.* Charlie's still talking and I'm having a hard time concentrating on her words.

"It's not just the key though. The docs figure your body adapted to your safe world so much that it's having trouble reverting back to Prime at the same time that it's trying to heal. Lucky you though, they're planning on letting you tag along with me back to your mirror branches for a bit." She stops and clarifies when she notices the pathetic hope blooming on my face. "Not your world, David. You can't go that far. If you want to keep your family safe, we've got to keep it sealed off, but we can set you up with a few odd jobs somewhere closer to it. Nothing heavy, just some light administrative work so you can recuperate somewhere similar to the place where you grew up. Give your body a chance to adjust, you know?"

Like mountain climbers tackling Everest in stages. Right now, I'd have trouble climbing out of the bed.

"Don't worry." Charlie walks back over and pats the back of my hand. "Few more IDOCS sessions and you'll be right as rain. Just ask the doctors to put you under if you hate them so much. You'll wake up and not remember a thing."

No. Nope. Hell no. As much as I hate feeling the things *in* me, the black sleep the sedative induces is worse, so much worse. "Please, no," I say with enough desperation that Charlie frowns down at me with sharp concern in her eyes. "Donlettem put me asleep. I wanna go home." I sound like a two-year-old. I feel like one. *Stray puppy.* That's all I am to her, some unplanned rescue she has to deal with before she gets back to her regular life—the one she's told me nothing about in our two weeks trapped here together. I'm slipping away. I can feel it and it terrifies me. It's a feedback loop. The more I panic, the faster the IDOCS pump tranquilizers into me. I try to grab Charlie's hand again, but mine isn't working anymore. "Doyou hava sister, a brother?" I ask before my throat closes. I want to ask her to help me, but I'm sinking too fast.

"Not here." She says and I see her touch one of her pearl earrings before my vision goes.

So, she's got one. In her safe world. Maybe that's who she goes and sees. And then the darkness swallows me up, thick and unescapable, like crashing through ice at midnight. This time though, it's different. This time, I fall through the other side, lungs burning, eyes bulging, into a dream.

It's James. I dream about James. He's packing for trade school. He's holding a gift for me.

Chapter Four

Today, the doctors declared me stable enough to transfer off-world to continue my healing. The Embassy doesn't want to let me out of their grip because they still haven't figured out how I broke my bridge or survived away from Prime so long. If they can replicate me, they can corral maneaters more effectively, extend reconnaissance missions, but they can't use me as a war weapon if I'm dead, and I must have gotten pretty close, because they're scared enough to send me somewhere closer to my safe world to convalesce. Like doctors of old prescribing trips to the seaside to improve one's constitution. Apparently, I'm Prime's equivalent of an 18th century invalid.

Eighteen days. Charlie has been here with me for eighteen days and six IDOCS treatments that I know of. That's all it took to change things, to make me go from not wanting to be seen by anyone at all, to not wanting to be seen by anyone ... except her. I've never been so vulnerable with someone in my entire life. I've spilled my guts. Literally and figuratively. Told her my whole life story—which is probably exactly why the Embassy kept her in containment with me far past the deadline of her own quarantine. Lonely, invisible teenage boys open up way more to pretty girls than thugs in suits with guns. Go figure.

As the plexiglass globe chugs into an upward revolution, the two doctors with access keys grin at us, looking insubstantial without their hazmat suits on. Something cold flickers in my stomach. *I'm in a foreign world, in the future. I've been here for half a month, and all I've seen of it is the inside of a fishbowl. Why does this feel like walking the plank instead of getting closer to home?*

"Chin up, Sunshine." Charlie bumps her shoulder against mine. "It's binge day not a beheading."

Binge day is what gatekeepers call their first day out of quarantine. Twelve hours reserved for getting the taste of vacuum-packed med meals out of your mouth by inhaling as much street food as you possibly could—and another twelve hours to recover from the ordeal and sleep in a real bed that wasn't within arms reach of a communal toilet. Although we won't be staying in Prime that long, Charlie has been adamant that I at least sample her favourite: smoked rat on a stick. "With pepper and lime dip, it's to die for. Or toasted tarmes with black lava salt." Tarmes are a large type of white grub that we don't have in the branch I grew up in. See, we really did talk about everything. Charlie knows more about me than anyone else in this world.

And I know what her favourite rodent and insect delicacies are. Score.

"I don't think I can eat." My ears are ringing. I still feel sick and that likely won't change until we get off world. I try not to lean on her as I duck through the portal and navigate the steps down to the warehouse floor, but my stitched leg aches, and I haven't done much walking these past weeks. I'm simultaneously grateful and embarrassed that Charlie is gripping my elbow.

The air is colder out here, and it smells different, like sawdust, sea water and the chalky, ammonia tinge of bird droppings. There's something else I can't place. Maybe worlds have their own unique smell, like lived-in houses do. Maybe I'm smelling rat on a stick.

"Don't be a stranger." The older, balding doctor winks at Charlie as he hands her a duffle bag. She pastes an obviously fake smile on her face and nods as she accepts it but rolls her eyes as soon as we push past the threadbare tarp.

"Great, now I've lost my appetite," she whispers in my ear.

"A doctor, Charlie. What a catch," I murmur back. "Don't let me hold you back. I can tell him you need a full physical, stat."

"Shut up," she says. And I do because I can't quite process what I'm seeing. It's another tarped-in partition with a hamster ball inside, just like ours. This one is unoccupied, with the beds tightly made and a handprint smearing the dust coating the plexiglass globe. I gawk and swallow as we walk by it.

Charlie sweeps aside another crinkly tarp. We stride past another empty pod.

"How many of these are there?" I ask.

"In here? Twenty, thirty maybe? There're other warehouses in other cities. The Embassy likes to keep its quarantine units separated from residential areas. Most people aren't super comfortable with potential off-world diseases as their next-door neighbors, so we're usually tucked away somewhere real nice like this."

"Are any of them being used right now?" Over the course of my stay, there had been times I had screamed. Quite a few times. I'd assumed we were alone in an abandoned building. I don't know why, but it feels more intrusive realizing that someone other than Charlie might have heard me. *You were on camera the whole time. God knows who heard you at your worst.*

"Dunno." Charlie shrugs. "Probably. The Embassy's current quarantine guest list—that's way above my pay grade. Gatekeepers only get need-to-know info. Come on." She shifts the bag on her shoulder and pulls me further. We're following a trail of other footprints through the dust.

So, no jails, but plenty of opportunities for death row as a keystone mule. Also warehouses full of hidden quarantine pods that the Embassy can fill with occupants as it pleases. Got it. *Who in the hell is this Embassy anyways?* I wonder, not for the first time. When am I going to be dragged in front of a hologram of an ominous, hooded man? I don't know which scares me more right now, faceless sinister evil, or the fact that Charlie is trying to convince me to eat bugs, and she's stronger than me. She could make me do it.

We exit the maze of tarped-in cubicles and head towards a huge roll-away door that's already open a crack. The sky glows a strange neon blue beyond. I shiver as we step out onto a crumbling pavement apron across from a marina boardwalk. Pale moths bob around our heads. Black water slaps against broad mooring posts across the road, and far across the bay, crowding the shoreline, is a sprawling, blindingly bright city.

Soaring metal standards with racks of fat stadium bulbs glare down on the streets in regimented rows. The night sky is bleached above them, a pale blue diffusion obscuring any stars that might be beyond. Obelisk shaped high-rises bristle with bright dashes and dots of glaring illumination, like towering rows of morse code scrolling up into the ashen night. Architectural beams and arches are highlighted with strip lighting. Every surface that isn't glass is underlit in green, blue, or white.

I've seen pictures of Las Vegas before, the flamboyant neon strips and bold marquee signs all vying for attention. This isn't like that. This is a city afraid of the dark. This is a place that banishes shadows because it knows that what likes to hide there is not the stuff of childhood nightmares but something tangible that's coming for them. This is an enormous flashlight under the blankets. The afterimage of the skyline burns behind my eyelids when I blink.

"What's it called?" I stare at the city's shattered reflection in the water. It's easier to take in in pieces.

"Scientia. It used to be the capital when this place was its own country." Charlie peers up the road that leads from the marina. She's waiting for something, so I say:

"It's pretty."

"It's a shithole."

I scuff my feet, trying to find my own balance without her help. "Better than a hamster ball with an IDOCS up my asshole?"

She snorts and smiles crookedly, and I add it to the mental tally of times I've made her laugh.

Stop it. She's not stuck in a cell with you anymore, and she's going to drop you the first chance she gets. You were pathetic in there.

"Better than IDOCS. Marginally." Charlie cranes her neck at a car rolling to a stop at the far end of the road and I try not to stare at the hollow between her collar bones. "Piece of junk is lost." She shifts the bag on her shoulder and fishes a palm sized disc out of her pocket, jabbing the screen several times. Text flashes across it.

The car's headlights flash twice, and it ambles towards us, bouncing and creaking over the ruts in the road. It's European looking. A sedan with a no-nonsense squared off body that is covered in graffiti. Its driver's side rear door is missing and a trail of damage along the side of the vehicle implies that it was sheared off at speed. There's no driver—not even a steering wheel—but the car eases to a stop before us easily enough, electric motor whirring. Something is sticking out of the sidewall of the tire closest to me—which is not made of rubber. Instead, the rim is encased in a network of braided together metal cable. A large knife has been jammed between the alloy strands, buried up to its hilt in the sidewall. "Fancy." I whistle. "Self-driving?"

"Barely."

"Yours?" It's hard to picture Charlie owning anything other than a motorcycle.

"Don't insult me. It's a taxi. Get in or you're walking."

I duck into the back and ease down carefully onto the cracked vinyl bench. It smells faintly of urine. Charlie peels open the front door, tosses her bag in, and drops down with a sharp sigh. A puff of dust rises around her and flecks of disintegrated yellow foam settle into her tightly-curled hair. I almost reach my hand out to brush them off. *Like you know her well enough to touch her hair.* My ears burn and I drop my gaze. There's a deflated condom wadded up by my foot. Mouse droppings litter the crusted floor mats. Mom would lose her mind. She hates mice.

A memory swamps me: Madeline with a dust mask pinching her face, clearing my whole family out of the seemingly mold infested cottage, pausing in the frenzy to have an ill-timed heart-to-heart with me. *'I just can't seem to get across the gap to you, and it hurts when you can't reach someone you love, David.'* An ache settles into my chest. She'd felt it all along, the gulf between us. I was a proxy of a son, not hers. I'm a stand-in for Charlie too, someone she's pretending to like because it's her job. But damned if she isn't good at it.

A distorted digital voice from the dash says "Ensure all passengers are seated. Ready for departure."

Charlie turns to face me as the car chimes three times and eases into reverse. "Don't touch anything." She pulls a small bottle out of her duffle bag and spritzes her hands. The sharp smell of rubbing alcohol fills the cab. "Hands?" I hold my palms out and she sprays them. "First impressions?" There's laughter in her voice.

The hand sanitizer stings a pinprick on the back of my hand where the IDOCS injected something. I don't know what. I peel my gaze from the pavement scrolling by and try not to think about how much it would hurt tipping out of the open door. "I hope you didn't pay full price for this."

"Do you always make bad jokes when you're scared?" Her voice softens and I glance up trying to gauge if she's making fun of me. She's not.

"Kind of perpetually, lately. Yeah." I rub my palms down my thighs.

"No need to be scared. You're tough. You made it through quarantine, and I only beat your ass in snakes and ladders a couple of times."

"Don't patronize me." I meant for that to come out in a different tone. I meant to keep joking with her, but the smell of alcohol burns my nostrils and stirs nausea in my belly.

"I'm not." Her voice is even quieter now.

"You don't have to pretend you like this ... that you like being stuck with me. Okay? We're out now." I'm being a jerk, I know it. I'm supposed to be cultivating a closeness with her, so she'll help me find my way back home. But my mind feels overloaded and impossible to regulate. Everything is too bright and smells too ghastly. This filthy car is the first time we've been alone without someone monitoring our every move—unless Charlie's wearing some sort of a wire. It's grating that she's still smoothing my ruffled feathers, like she's been ordered to pacify me.

She straightens and all the softness falls from her face, revealing something sharper beneath. "Maybe I actually do like it. Like *you*. You ever stop to consider that, Sunshine?"

"You give all your stray puppies nicknames, or just your favourites?" I snap. *Jesus, what are you doing? First time in two weeks you can express emotion without an eye in the sky watching you, and you turn on her, of all people?*

She's here. No-one else is.

She swallows. "I'm sorry I called you a stray puppy."

"They've ordered you to babysit me, haven't they? The Embassy. They're pissed that their precious asset is too fragile to keep here under glass, and they want to keep tabs on me. They're making you do it because you crossed them somehow. That's why they kept you in quarantine longer. That, and they wanted me to think we *bonded* on the inside, right Charlie? I've spilled my guts to you all drugged up, and now I'm supposed to be convinced that we've got the start of something *real*, right? So, be real with me for one Goddamned second, okay? Why you? What did you do to rile up your bosses so much that they sidelined your whole life to stick you with me?"

She shakes her head and turns away. There's no rear-view mirror so I can't see her expression. "First of all, stop with this bullshit that you're not worth anyone's time just because you've used invisibility as a survival skill your whole life. Secondly, why *me*? I'm *here,* David. I'm convenient. That's all the qualification the Embassy needs. There's not exactly a big talent pool to choose from. Mass suicide and murder as a tactic in a generational war tends to thin out a population. And we're not allowed to work off world without partners. You need off-world, and I need a partner. Simple as that."

"You didn't have a partner when you found me."

"Gold star. Very observant." Sarcasm sours her words.

The car keeps backing up, hitting potholes with gusto. I want to reach out and grab something to avoid hitting the roof, but I don't want to touch anything either.

Oh shit. The realization hits me. "You weren't supposed to be there. You weren't on an official job when you found me?"

"I wasn't."

I swallow hard before asking "Why don't you have a partner, Charlie?"

"He died." Her voice shakes.

Oh shit. "On the job?"

She nods. "Couple trips before yours. We take turns. He was the primitus keystone on that run, and things went south. We had dark walkers swamping us. I had to close the gate and he was still on the wrong side..." She fades off. Tendons stand out on her neck.

The car stops and turns toward the city. The cracked windshield tints automatically in the glare of the lights ahead.

Charlie shrugs. "So, yeah, I'm being reprimanded. But pardon me if I'm alright being sidelined to babysit. Take you on a couple milk runs to a reasonably safe branch? I'm all over it. Grab you by the hand

and baby-step you through the basics because we don't have enough manpower for anyone—even the Embassy's newest chosen one—not to pull their weight? You'd better believe I volunteer. Handle you with kid gloves and stroke your fragile ego, so you don't break down in my care? Hell yes. Sign me up. You're a job, David. Is that what you wanted to hear? But you're a job I asked for, so don't talk to me like I'm some sort of brainwashed lick-your-boots lackey who didn't risk my neck to save your *fucking life*. Because—trust me—if I didn't want to be stuck with you, I could have left you under that couch for the dark walkers to pull apart, and no-one would have known any different. Prime wouldn't even know you existed. Now, are we done feeling fucking sorry for ourselves? Because I'm hungry."

I don't say anything. I just sit there with the wind whipping my hair against my cheeks and raising goosebumps on my skin. There's something wrong with me because I feel better now that I got her to break and swear at me. The pressure in my chest eases. This is Charlie talking to me now. Not an Embassy mouthpiece, not a careful young woman who considered every word while imprisoned alongside a stranger. Just Charlie. Unfiltered. I want more of it. I want to feel her hand in mine again. I want that shiver to sweep down my spine when she laughs. I want ... I want this closeness to be real.

Oh God, I'm going to eat rat on a stick for her, aren't I?

Chapter Five

The taxi drops us off on a crowded market street. The people here glow. I'm not talking healthy skin. They wear jewelry that lights up, chunky bangles and pendant necklaces that pulse with seizure-inducing flashes. Strings of pinpoint pearls twist through elaborately braided hair. Some of them have lights under their skin, IDOCS installed, I presume. We pass a man in a red fishnet vest with obscenely big biceps. Illumination radiates through his upper arms, like someone buried bands of red-hot iron there. A woman leans close to her friend, coloured hexagon patterns scurrying across her cheekbones, mimicking the ones on her companion's face. They remind me of cuttlefish. I'm sure there's more to take in, but the market is insanely overstimulating.

Everything is so intensely lit that afterimages eat holes in my field of vision. The vendor stalls are underlit and molded white acrylic, same as the floor of the hamster ball. Aromas swim through the thick air, frying fish, hot peppers, and floral perfumes with astringent undertones. Skyscrapers loom on either side of the boulevard, but the market is boxed in by a latticework canopy scrolling digital advertisements over our heads like the opening to *Star Wars*. I catch ads for shoes, gum, battery banks, cigarettes, and what looks like an anime for some sort of penis enhancement device. That looks to be a thing here, fashion-wise. Just about every dude we jostle past is sporting a lit-up codpiece like it's a landing strip for their cock. I've never been so happy to be out of style.

I don't recognize half the things for sale on the tables. We push through clotted people and rows of trayed food that look like building blocks. Some sort of milky drink with live bugs in it. The entire crowd is yelling at the top of their lungs. Hawkers, customers, everyone. I feel like the only sober person at a hardcore rave. Charlie shouts something as she steers me through people soup, but I can't hear her. I'm shutting down.

By the time we pile into the narrow hallway of a used-up apartment building, my teeth hurt from clamping them and my ears are ringing again.

"You okay?" She asks breathlessly as she pulls me up a set of stairs. She's holding my hand again and I don't know when she grabbed it.

"That was ... a lot."

"Yeah, the Pot is a bit much sometimes. You can chill in the room, and I'll go back and get us something to eat."

"Your place?" I ask as she stops in front of a green apartment door that looks like it was painted in a hurry. There are screw holes with long paint drips where the numbers used to hang.

"Gatekeeper quarters. We don't have our own permanent housing. Job's too migratory." She holds the disc tablet up to the door and a lock clicks.

Inside looks like a college dorm room, all spartan, mismatched furniture, dented appliances, and threadbare carpet. There's the faint smell of stale beer, but otherwise, it's tidy with scrubbed counters and vacuumed floors. A brand-new pair of huge running shoes sit lined up on a rubber mat by the door. A big guy with a beard reclines on the couch, frowning down at a disc tablet balanced on his legs.

"Hey, Cory," Charlie says. "Been back long?"

"Couple weeks. Lee's doing another stint in recoup so I'm back in the partner pool, it seems. Didn't think you'd be back out with just a hand slap..." He fades off as he looks up and sees me. For a moment, it feels like I'm in the crosshairs of a bull who's about to charge, but then the guy's cheeks bunch, and he lets out a deep belly laugh that fills up the whole room. "Holy shit. This him?"

"Be nice." Charlie drops the duffle bag.

"I'm always nice." He laughs again, like I'm the punchline of a particularly delightful joke. Then he sets his tablet aside, wipes his eyes, and stands up smoothing down a tailored polo shirt. "I'd have dressed up if I knew we were having royalty over."

"No codpiece?" The words are out of me before I can take them back.

Cory freezes and looks me up and down before grinning and waggling a finger. "I like this one, Charlie."

"David, this is Cory Proust. He's a pathologist and a cataloger. We'll be working with him for the next couple of weeks. You'll be his field assistant."

"N-nice to meet you. David Rawlinson." I hold my sweaty hand out and Cory vice-grips it, watching to see if I wince. I don't. *Great. Thirty seconds in, and we're in a pissing contest. I don't have the bandwidth for this right now.*

"Sorry about Lee. Bad this time?" Charlie draws the conversation back to her.

"Bad enough. You know how it is with the front-line crowd. I'd crack too if the bastards made me watch worlds end." Cory waves his hands dismissively. "He's where he needs to be. That's what matters. Let's hope he gets something out of it this time."

"You eat?" she asks.

"Not yet."

"What can I get you?"

"The regular."

"David, how about you? Hungry?"

It takes me a moment to realize she's talking to me. I feel like I'm half a second behind the rest of the room, mired in agitation. "No thanks. Could I, uh … I just really need a smoke. Cigarettes. I saw an ad. You have cigarettes here, right?"

"Goddamn, I'd kill myself if we didn't." The big man shoulders past me, opens the bi-fold coat closet door and rifles through the pockets of a thick overcoat, pulling out a pack of smokes and a stainless-steel lighter. "On me. Happy binge day. There's an ashtray on the balcony." He thumbs toward the narrow window beside the couch.

"Thank you." I slide a filtered cigarette out of the tidy rows and clutch the lighter. It's cold and grounding in my hand. I've always been a recreational smoker. A craving's never hit me this hard before. It feels like my brain is exposed and some small animal is licking it, about to take a bite out of me. I fumble with the window latch and spill out onto a half balcony. Behind me, I hear Cory mutter, "He looks like death warmed over. We better move fast."

Charlie snaps, "Shut up."

I don't care. All that matters right now is the smell of struck flint, that first puff of smoke filling my nostrils and nicotine tingling through me.

The balcony is all chipped tiles and mildew corners. It opens onto a narrow alley with rows of identical platforms. Light still blazes back here, but it's softer and more diffuse than the boulevard was. A cool breeze that smells like damp bricks and garbage wafts up the back street and the incandescent noise of the market reaches here, but it's muted.

The first few drags loosen my ribcage and ease the tension in my neck. I take my weight off my sore leg and blink down at the pavement below. My mind feels full of static. Am I really from here? Some psychedelic sci-fi city that never sleeps? I don't feel like I am. *Then why the hell were you invisible in your world and people here see you just fine?* The cruel thought lances through me.

Cory steps out onto the ledge beside me and I have to press my hip against the concrete half wall so that we both fit out here. I'm suddenly gripped by the idea of him throwing me over the rail, my head cracking open as I smack the ground, my brains glistening in the false light. *Jesus, what's wrong with you?*

He pokes a cigarette between his lips and holds out his hand for the lighter. I pass it over wordlessly. For several breaths we stand there, squinting down at the alley, flicking ashes, and blowing smoke into the night.

"You go to school?" He asks without turning to me.

I nod.

"How long's formal education in your world?"

"Depends on if you go to college or university. I was supposed to graduate high school this year."

"How old are you?"

"Almost eighteen," I say.

"Ever hold down a job?"

Christ, he sounds like my dad, but he's younger, somewhere close to James's age. "Flipping burgers and making ice cream cones."

"This is going to be different than that."

No shit. He doesn't say anything else, so I glance at him as I smoke. He's got a soft face, but he wears it as armor. His eyes are hard. The skin on his hands is chapped and cracked. "Charlie said you're a pathologist? You study disease?" I ask.

"And I perform necropsies." I don't know what that means, and it must show on my face because he adds: "I dissect animals and you're going to help me. Hope you're not squeamish."

"What sort of animals?"

He crushes out his cigarette on the railing. "Dark walkers."

I completely shut down after that. I don't remember much other than going to a bedroom with a door and no cameras above me. If I'm not too loud, I can hyperventilate as much as I want. There're no witnesses. No light switches in the room either. Once I'm through the throes of an excruciating panic attack, heart still thunking in my chest and tinnitus pinging between my ears, I look for a toggle, dial or button, but there's only a narrow bed, an overhead light, and me. No nightstand, no furniture. And no light switch or pull chain. It doesn't hit me until I notice an assortment of sleep masks lined up beside the pillow. *Shit. They never turn off the lights when they sleep.* I thought it was just some annoying observation protocol while we were in the hamster ball, but no. The whole damned city—probably the whole world—goes to bed with the lights on.

I pick out a blue sleep mask. When I fall asleep, I dream of James again. Same dream. Him giving me an early birthday gift. God, I miss him. I miss my whole family. They've never felt so far away.

On the train out of Scientia city, Charlie runs through what our field trip will look like. "Two weeks in the branches closest to your safe world. They're all infested, but don't worry, we're only visiting recently razed worlds. The dark walkers there will be sluggish. They aren't particularly interested in hunting. Think of them like lions who just made a big kill. They won't bother us. And they won't come out in the daylight. We've got enough light packs with us to shelter overnight if we have to, but we plan to spend our nights in uninfected dimensions. Like I said, it's a milk run," she assures me. "We're just there to give you a chance to heal up properly and collect any keystones and tickets we can find."

"Speak for yourself," Cory says. He's hunched on the bench seat across from us, but he's big enough that his knees nearly brush mine.

The guy doesn't look built for public transportation. "I'm there to cut stuff up." The bag he packed this morning looked like he was planning a mass murder, all hacksaws and bolt cutters, reciprocating saws and scalpels. *Don't get on the wrong side of this guy,* I think for the hundredth time.

The train takes us out of the city, past abandoned towns with crumbling buildings to an end-of-the-line station that's merely a platform with an awning shade, a bulk tote with the label *potable water* stamped on it, and a row of rusty bicycles lined up in a bike stand. Desiccated wheat fields stretch as far as I can see.

Charlie hands me a wide brimmed hat. We fill up three large water bottles from the tank, shoulder our duffle bags, and follow a narrow dirt trail for about a kilometer. It feels like a marathon. It's hot out. The sun seems bigger here, and the water from my bottle is warm and tastes like plastic. My leg hurts, and my limbs feel rubbery and unreliable.

"Take it slow," Charlie tells me. "Tell us if you need to stop."

Cory just keeps glancing at me warily, like I'll drop dead where I stand if he doesn't keep tabs. I must really look like shit.

We pass a pair of armed guards flanking a bridge over a creek. Charlie flashes her disc tablet as we pass, and they nod back. And then we arrive at what looks like a bomb shelter, a knoll protruding out of the yellow plains, all reinforced concrete entrances, metal doors and squat chimneys. We stand in front of a camera for several seconds before the door clunks, groans, and chugs open. Four soldiers escort us down a white circular corridor made of ribbed metal. It reminds me of the time Jord and Jess dared me to climb through the culvert in the ditch on the way to school one morning.

I got stuck and my twin brothers forgot me there. Assholes.

Anyways. The bunker creeps me out. I'm consumed by this ridiculous certainty that I'll never see the sky again. We go through several sets of doors with keypad locks requiring lengthy codes. Every time a new one opens, the tinny squeal cutting through my head gathers volume. I'm pretty sure no-one else hears it. No-one's wincing like I am anyways. Jesus, I've never had tinnitus this bad.

Stretching my jaw, I try to pop my ears, but the shrill feedback doesn't diminish.

The soldiers usher us into an oval shaped room containing nothing but a faded blue car surrounded by a black and yellow hashmark boundary stencilled onto the floor. Like the vehicle is biohazardous.

The squealing in my head crescendos. I blink at the car. I don't know what I was expecting down here, but this wasn't it. Squinting at the emblem on the trunk I mumble, "Toyota Corolla?"

"Yup." Charlie presses her thumb against one of the soldier's disc tablets and it beeps.

"W-why?" I ask. How the hell did it even get in here? None of the hallways we used are big enough to drive a vehicle through.

"Over 50 million of them sold in your dimension alone." Cory answers like he's a used car salesman.

The two soldiers at the rear hold up an armored case between them and tap their fobs against its latches. "Primitus?" one of them asks, impassive gaze shifting between Charlie and Cory.

"Me," Charlie says.

"Hang on." Another soldier enters the room behind us, boots clacking. He holds out a crisp sheet of folded paper. Beneath the brim of his patrol cap, his eyes are so dark, they're almost black and the angles of his face are as sharp as cut glass. "Ma'am, apologies. Orders came down the line this morning. Your roster's been updated and I'm primitus for this run." He doesn't sound sorry at all as he hands Charlie the paper and stands at attention while she scans it.

"Perfect," Cory sighs. "Just what we were missing, a token grunt. Military can't keep its fingers out of anything."

Charlie's face pinches as she reads, but her voice is unruffled. "Whatever. Knock yourself out, champ." She steps aside and gestures the soldier forward.

He approaches his compatriots, holds his thumb out and presses it against a scanner on the front of the armored case. It clicks open.

The squealing leaps to a higher pitch that feels like knitting needles skewering my brain through my ears. I suck breath through my teeth hard enough that Charlie turns to me, concern pooling in her eyes.

"You okay?"

I can barely hear her over the resonance cutting through my skull, but I nod because that's what guys do when freaky shit happens that they can't explain. Pretend everything's fine.

Our primitus pulls a zippered orange pouch from the armored case.

That's where the noise is coming from. Whatever is in there. Jesus, it's horrible, like fingernails on chalk distilled down to a deeply unsettling resonance in my bones, like something capable of breaking me from the inside. Is no-one else hearing this?

I glance at faces as the soldier sorts through several small objects inside the pouch before plucking one of them out.

It's a set of car keys.

No-one else is reacting to the godawful sound of them. No-one else can hear it. Maybe I'm dying? Having an aneurysm? What are the symptoms of something like that?

A kid who looks way too young to be in uniform opens the driver's side door and then steps back so that his toes are behind the border on the floor. Inside the car, there's blood on the upholstery. Lots of it. Old, the colour of rust, staining the seat cushions and crusting the floor mats, like someone died in there ... or birthed something out.

I swallow hard.

This is what gets me one step closer to my family. This is our gateway. People have crossed it bleeding. Multiple people by the looks of it.

Chapter Six

"Inventory, please." The new addition to our party prompts Charlie and she taps her tablet against his. He reads out loud. "One digital assistant."

"Confirmed," Charlie says.

"One standard issue pulsed laser handgun."

"Confirmed," Charlie says.

"One field journal."

"Confirmed."

"Two high-capacity power stations and two foldable LED panels."

"Confirmed and confirmed."

"One keystone detector."

"Confirmed."

It goes on like this. This guy. He's going to be a riot to travel with. I can tell already.

We all stand there waiting as he lists everything in Charlie's duffle bag including underwear, socks, and feminine hygiene products—even her pearl earrings. She verifies each item. At the bottom of her list are several changes of clothes and hygiene items for me. I don't have my own bag. Like a kid who's not trustworthy enough to pack for a sleepover.

Cory confirms everything he's packed next. His list sounds like a mash up of a butcher shop, morgue, and science lab.

The soldier says something I can't hear over the ringing and then looks pointedly at me.

Shit. "What?"

"Inventory?" He enunciates the word crisply.

"I—uh—don't have anything except what I'm wearing."

"Nothing in your pockets? No currency, piercings, jewelry, hair elastics, smoking paraphernalia, medical patches, bandages, loose buttons, or snaps?" He rattles it off like he's said it a million times.

"Uh. I don't think so." I awkwardly check my pockets as I say it. These aren't my pants. I don't know what happened to the clothes I showed up in, but the Embassy procured multiple pairs of pants cut the same as my old jeans and several t-shirts replicating the one I'd been wearing when Charlie saved me, complete with a faded AC/DC logo. I guess that's my uniform now.

"Anything in your pockets? Yes or no," the soldier prompts impatiently.

"He's good, Riley. I'll vouch for him." Charlie pats the guy's shoulder, and he looks pissed, but nods.

"Inventory confirmed." He nods like we should all be satisfied with the proclamation. Then he strides past the kid holding open the Corolla's door and hoists himself into the driver's seat, heedless of the blood stains. I watch as he effortlessly clears the centre console and shifts to the passenger seat. He's got at least three guns on him. Shoulder holster. Hip. Thigh. And he moves like he was born wearing this gear.

"Proceed," he says curtly from his seat, car keys and orange zippered bag still in hand. Those black eyes pin Charlie with an expectant gaze.

She opens the rear door and wrinkles her nose. The upholstered bench seat is stained horribly too, a black hole of old blood oozing over the edge of the middle cushion and onto the floor. Charlie climbs past it. "Would it kill you guys to clean up a bit?" Perching against the passenger door, she pulls her duffle bag onto her lap.

"We're under orders to keep the gateway clear at all times, Ma'am," Tight Ass replies from the front seat. "No entry allowed unless it's pre-approved. Sirs?" He turns to us.

Charlie waves me in first, so I awkwardly climb in beside her doing my best to ignore the awful stain between us. The coltish soldier outside closes the door behind me and then practically leaps back into position toeing the hash-marked boundary.

Cory takes a towel out of his bag and gingerly sets it on the soiled driver's seat before gripping the steering wheel and swinging in. The car rocks on its shocks as he sits down.

"You're taking that through with us." Tight Ass points at the corner of the towel under Cory's rear. "No mistakes on my missions."

"You're a mistake, Riley," the big man snaps.

"Whoa, I've got it. Ignore him." Charlie leans ahead and shoots the soldier a winning grin. "I'll verify inventory matches up when we come home." That's when I realize why this is all so meticulous. Anything we inadvertently leave behind on our trip would become a keystone. When Tight Ass Riley doesn't answer, she says, "We're all cozy and ready to go, if you are."

"Time?" He barks to the soldier still holding the driver's door open like he's our personal valet.

"0432, Sir."

"0432 confirmed." He grabs the short brim of his hat and announces "Every light lit. Nothing left behind." Then he leans over and jams the keys into the ignition.

"Every light lit. Nothing left behind." The mantra echoes off the walls as everyone outside the vehicle repeats it. The young soldier closes the driver's door.

He vanishes when the latch clicks. So does everyone else in the room. It's so sudden that my mind has trouble processing it. There are afterimages of the men, hazy silhouettes of where they stood, and then nothing.

"Holy shit," I say. I think my vision is blurring, but then realize that the windshield is filmy with dust.

"Nothing holy about it," Cory chuckles from up front, but it's an uncomfortable noise.

Riley pulls the keys from the ignition and deposits them in the orange bag before handing it to Cory. Then he takes a handgun out and tells us all to wait. The door groans loudly as he opens it and the agonized echo of it fills the hollow room.

"Is this it?" I ask, neck prickling as I peer through the grimy windows while the soldier methodically clears the room. It's not well lit here, not like the room we just left behind, and that's raising alarm bells in my head of an entirely different kind.

Maneaters hide in the dark.

"Is this the world we're working in? Nah," Cory says. "This one's empty. He's just a damned stickler about following protocol. The routes we take ensure there are plenty of buffer dimensions between us and the dark walkers. Embassy wouldn't risk Prime by opening a direct route to an infected world. According to the route map for this run, we've got four more gates to hopscotch before we get to the one we're aiming for."

Four more jumps closer to my family.

"I babysat him when he was a kid and he was a runny-nosed little prick," Charlie mutters to Cory.

"Riley?" he says and then snorts. "I worked with his dad. The asshole doesn't fall far from the tree."

I can't make sense of any of that. Riley is noticeably older and bigger than Charlie. She'd said she babysat him when he was a *kid*. I must have misheard.

"Clear," Riley says, and we pile out of the Corolla. Cory gives him back the ticket bag and he tucks it into a zippered pocket beneath his armored vest.

We leave the decrepit bunker and walk several kilometres along a twisted broken railway until we reach an abandoned town. This hike doesn't feel as tiring as the first. When we reach a grocery store with busted windows and garbage-strewn shopping carts still dutifully lined-up and locked in their return stalls, Riley pulls the orange pouch out and fishes out a metal token. He feeds it into one of the cart handles, hands the bag back to Cory, and pushes the cart toward the entrance. Its wheels shudder over the broken pavement. We follow him to a jammed sliding door with a faded picture of bananas on it. Before we cross the threshold, Riley takes out his gun, and Charlie takes out hers too. A natural movement, like they've partnered like this before.

I don't know why that makes me jealous.

Cory asks, "Long wait or little one?"

"Uh, long one I think," she says. Then Riley and she are gone. Just blotted from existence.

The ringing in my ears drops a notch. My heart seizes and my mind lurches. I know she just went through another gateway, but my limbic system doesn't get that. It surges into fight-or-flight mode and my breathing hangs up loud enough for Cory to hear it.

"Don't worry. Seeing someone blip, it's not natural and your body knows it. Everyone glitches a bit on their first few passages. You'll get your dimensional legs under you yet." His voice is kind, deep, and naturally warm. Right now, he seems like the kind of guy that you'd go to for advice, and you'd implicitly trust whatever he told you.

"This is insane," I rasp. "What if something comes at them in there?"

"That's what her dipshit military guard is for." Cory smiles lopsidedly. He holds up the orange bag containing all the other tickets. "We're their reserve. If something happens that they can't handle, we go back the way we came and make sure everything closes behind us. Standard procedure. The primitus opens the gateways and reconnoitres. The reserve holds the tickets and waits for the all-clear."

"What if I go in after her?" I don't know why I say it, or why it comes out so desperate. I guess Charlie is my only anchor in this craziness and I haven't been away from her yet.

"All chivalrous-like? She sure as shit doesn't need you and I'd slit your throat before you ever got close enough to try it," he says. Just like that, all the warmth in him is gone.

Jesus Christ, I can't get a read on this guy.

"I don't jack off to the Embassy handbook like Glory Boy in there," Cory continues. "But I won't let you compromise procedure out here, kid. It'd put the whole damned universe in danger." He wanders over to a cement barricade and sighs as he eases his bulk down. "So, how about you get comfy. We'll be here awhile."

"It only took him a second to clear the room with the Toyota."

"That's because we all blipped at the same time." He frowns. "Aw Jesus. No-one went over time dilation with you, did they?"

"What?" I gape.

"Figures." He guffaws like he just heard the best joke ever, and when he can speak again, he says, "Did she tell you anything at all while you two were stuck in that goldfish bowl?"

"She told me that your forefathers made a big knot in the universe and then opened a door to somewhere they shouldn't have." I scratch at the bandage below my knee. "And a bunch of venomous asshole aliens crashed the party and ate all the guests."

"She tell you what else it did, the Breach?" *The Breach.* An event so impactful, it changed how Prime measured time. Years were separated into *Before Breach* and *After Breach.* Everything revolved around first contact with the maneaters, the hellhounds, the dark walkers. Whatever you called them, the creatures first foray into this universe warped everything.

"She said it cocked everything up," I say, trying to ignore the squeal radiating from the orange bag he's holding.

Cory snorts. "Yeah. In a nutshell. We sewed so many connections together, snarled up so many branches. A knot like that has a resonance. It's loud in space. We screamed into the void and" —he grins like a madman. — "something heard us. A civilization from another tree. They breached through one of our far twig dimensions. Some sort of massive energy field surge accompanied the bastard's arrival. It fried some tickets and damaged others. Our military hit back hard and fast. Back then, the scout hoards were small enough to fend off. Word is, even in your branch, our ancestors ran successful push back campaigns."

I jerk. The idea of the maneaters on my side, pins me like cement setting in my stomach. "I-in *my* world?"

"Yeah. You're lucky, kid. Those were early encounters, and we were able to restrain and blockade them. Funny thing, your branch seems to be a port town for sinister invaders. Dark walkers weren't the first ones to get the idea. No. Seems like there're myths about people trying to bottle up a great evil all throughout your history, isn't there? We studied them in school. Satan confined to a bottomless pit. Gog and Magog. Fenrir the giant wolf. Koschei the Deathless. Prime thought those myths might give us some clues as to how the folks in your branch fended off invasions, but they weren't much help. Looks like you're our best bet yet. David, the door crasher."

"Fuck." The word spills out of me. This can't be real. I keep telling myself that. There's no way this is real, but it is. I'm sitting in a grocery store parking lot in a gutted dimension getting a history lesson from a burly guy who butchers aliens for a living. And the bag of tickets he's holding is screaming at me. "What's time dilation?" I gulp. Anything to take my mind off the noise.

"Come here." He fishes a coil-bound journal out of his bag and pats the spot beside him, but I'm not keen on sitting right now, so I pace.

This feels like the moment before you get bad news. When your stomach has already dropped and your neck's prickling because your body knows something awful is coming.

"Fine. At least come closer. It's easier if I draw it out." He pulls a pencil out from the coil and smooths out a sheet of graph paper. "Einstein figured it out in your world." He sketches a rough line drawing of what looks like a tree.

"Figured out what?" I glance at his drawing.

"If someone is standing still and someone else is moving really fast—like near light speed—time passes slower for the person going fast relative to the poor bloke who's not moving. Theory of relativity and all that. Your world knows of the Big Bang theory, yeah?"

"The universe exploding into existence? You my science teacher now?"

He smiles at that and draws a dot at the base of the tree. "Here's Prime. We figure we're the trunk of our universe, the base. So, think of Prime as the guy who's standing still." He traces his lead up the tree. "Everything else is expanding. All these branches are moving away from us at speeds that are getting really close to the speed of light, so time slows down relative to us the further up the limbs you go, understand? A few seconds up-tree translates to way, way longer down the trunk. Gateways let us hop into dimensions we could never reach otherwise, but time dilation affects us while we're there. When you crossed your bridge, did time move slower in your safe world, slower on the other side, or a mix of both?"

"Most of the time no time passed on my side."

He frowns just like the Embassy interviewer did. "Must have been some time passing. You sure?"

"Why does everybody keep asking me that?"

He holds up a hand placatingly. "Hang on. This is why we sketch

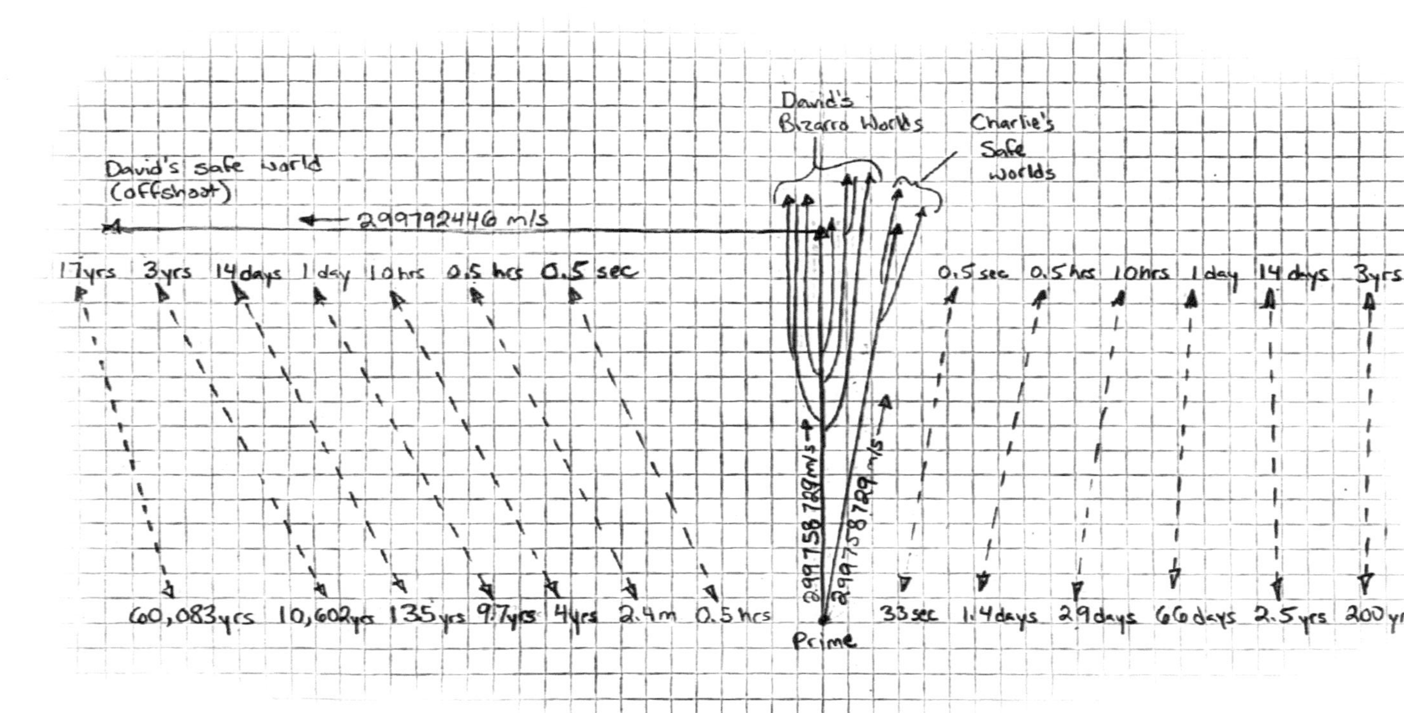

David's safe world (offshoot)
David's Bizarro Worlds
Charlie's Safe worlds
299792446 m/s
17yrs 3yrs 14days 1day 10hrs 0.5hrs 0.5sec
0.5sec 0.5hrs 10hrs 1day 14days 3yrs
299758729m/s
299758729m/s
60,083yrs 10,602yrs 135yrs 9.7yrs 4yrs 2.4m 0.5hrs
33sec 14days 29days 66days 2.5yrs 200yrs
Prime

things out." Rummaging through his bag, he pulls out his disc tablet. "Okay. You got a name for your mirror worlds?"

"Bizarro world." It sounds so stupid saying it out loud.

"I like it." He grins and labels the bunch of branches sprouting like a candelabra above the Prime dot: *David's Bizarro worlds*. Then he draws a twig further above them all and labels its point: *David's Safe World*. "Was there any time that you visited Bizarro worlds and noticed some time passing on your side?"

"If I spent all day away, about ten minutes would pass on my side."

"All day? Be more specific kid. How many hours away?"

I frown, remembering the long days I spent in Bizarro world trying to sort out how to save my family from the bridge I'd built to the maneaters. "Twelve hours."

He jots down some numbers. "And what's the longest span of time you spent away without any time passing on your side?"

"About half an hour."

"Right then, we'll assume for every half hour you spend in a Bizarro world, less than a second passes in your foster dimension. That close enough to what you remember?"

I nod.

"Let's say half a second just to give us a number to work with." Cory types something into his tablet.

"What are you doing?" I lean closer.

"There are equations for time dilation. I can plug in the numbers you gave me and estimate how fast your safe world is moving in relation to your Bizarro..." His forehead wrinkles as he squints at the output of the equation. "That can't be right."

"What is it?"

"Dimensions travel away from Prime at around 299,758,729 m/s. I mean, there are discrepancies among them. None of them are moving at *exactly* the same velocity, but they're pretty close."

"So?" I feel like I'm failing a test already. Like Cory is the hallowed mentor from one of those cheesy chosen one movies and I'm the kid who's trying to impress him and failing. Is it weird that I like the idea of him being a mentor? I've never had one except for James.

"So, according to this, your safe world is moving away from your Bizarro worlds at 299,792,446 m/s. That's some 30,000m/s faster than most dimensions."

"Doesn't seem like much."

"It is." Cory clamps his pencil in his teeth and speaks around it. "Time dilation is exponentially related to speed. There's no way your safe world should be moving like that unless ... holy shit. Unless it's an offshoot." He spits out the pencil, erases the line leading to *David's safe world* and instead draws a line perpendicular to the Bizarro worlds' branches. "Offshoots are different than branches. Faster and perpendicular to the trunk. We have no idea why they form or why they're faster. No-one's ever travelled to one... Oh my God. No wonder the Embassy is keeping you bubble-wrapped. Your foster world is an offshoot."

My head hurts. I can't keep track of this all. Running my fingers through my hair, I point at the top of the drawing. "So, all of these are moving faster than Prime. Time stretches out, slows down up-tree. Seconds passing in my world means way more time passes in the trunk, so people age faster in Prime anywhere else?"

"Yeah, kid." Cory says it quietly like he's talking to a horse who's ready to bolt.

"Riley," I blurt, looking toward the grocery store sliding doors. "Charlie said she babysat him when he was a kid. Like for real? She said we're only spending a couple weeks up here. How long is that for them down in Prime?"

"Two weeks is a typical shift for a gatekeeper. The headaches get bad if we stay up-tree longer than that. We're hopping around a bit so that we don't leave a bread crumb trail home, but most of the time it works out to somewhere between two to three years back home."

"T-three years?" My mouth dries out. I'm shaking my hands because my fingers are tingling. The ringing in my ears is relentless.

"How about you sit down now, yeah?" Cory says His voice is switched to warm mode again.

"Shit." I breathe. "Shit. No—that's not. That can't be right. Charlie was in her safe world for *three* years. She said her family came and brought her back to Prime. Her parent, the one who wasn't the primitus..."

"It wasn't her parent that came and fetched her. It was some cousin, niece or nephew three or four generations down the line. All the family she knew back home would have been long dead by then, you understand? Three years away is two hundred on Prime. That's why so many kids never came home, David. Families just died out and the war kept going. Gatekeepers don't have it much better. We try to repair the raggedy ass universe our ancestors left us, and we go home after work to a world getting older than us every damned time. Lee will have more wrinkles than when I left him."

My knees go out from under me. I'm sitting on the pavement with pebbles digging into the palms of my hands because the bomb has finally hit. Fuck. Fuck. Fuck me. "You said m-my world—my safe world—was going even faster. I was..." I swallow, taste bile, and try again. "I was away for seventeen years. The Enrils. The Embassy guys called me Mr. Enril."

Cory leans forward and grips my shoulder like he's afraid I'm about to sink through the pavement. "Sorry, kid. That's what they call all you lost ones. Expatriate No Record In Library. ENRIL."

"How long is seventeen years in Prime's time?"

"Too long, David." He shakes his head.

"Put it in your calculator, please."

He does and his face drops when he sees the result.

I lean toward him, and he pulls the tablet to his chest, but not fast enough. Snatching the device, I stare down at the numbers glowing on the glossy screen.

60,083 years.

"That can't be right." I shove the tablet back to Cory. "Do it again. You made a mistake." I watch him plug the numbers in this time. 17 years. 299792446 m/s. The result comes out the same.

60,083 years.

I can't breathe.

Cory murmurs, "Your folks are from Before Breach. They're our ancient ancestors. You've survived a hostile offshoot dimension for seventeen years. And you collapsed a bridge in a way no-one's ever done before. This is all uncharted territory, David. This is why the Embassy's pulling every string to make sure you keep living. Why they're willing to send you away while consequently losing years of researching you to make sure you pull through. No-one's ever seen anything like you."

A mess of panic, rage and fear balls up behind my sternum, cramming everything else up my throat. "No-one thought to ask me if I was okay with any of this *before* we started the trip?"

"Okay with what?" he says bluntly. "You were dying in Prime from what I heard. Acclimation sickness or some shit. The docs pumped you up with enough drugs to keep you alive until we could get you back up-tree. And I gotta be honest, you look like hot shit right now. You honestly telling me you've got the nerve to be pissed because we're trying to save you?"

No, I'm pissed because I'm scared shitless and this all seems massive, terrifying, and too heavy to bear. I'm pissed because I'm some prima-donna prodigal son for a world I don't even know. And because the goddamned noise won't stop. I didn't sign up for this. Not any of it.

Chapter Seven

Riley and Charlie blip back into existence hours later. The ringing in my ears has numbed me by then, but I still jump at the sight of them.

"It's good. Come on," Charlie says, so we go through.

Riley rolls the cart back to its corral, retrieves his token and takes the ticket bag.

"This is my garage world," Charlie says as we circle behind the grocery store, and I don't understand until we enter the loading dock office out back. The building's lone desk has been catapulted out the front door to make room for an orange and black KTM Duke 390. It leans on its kickstand on a floor littered with yellowed ledgers, crumpled chip bags and empty Tums bottles. A pair of dirt bikes are parked behind Charlie's ride. They look too small for Cory and Riley, but when Charlie navigates her motorcycle out the narrow entryway, the two men grab the helmets hanging on the smaller bikes' handlebars and steer the machines outside.

I ride bitch behind Charlie again. There's no room behind Cory or Riley, and even if there was, I'm happy to have a valid excuse to wrap my arms around her waist. I feel like I'll dissolve if I don't hang onto her. I'm lost. 60,000 years away from where I came from and worlds away from my family kind of lost. And Charlie seems like the only constant, the only anchor amidst a storm that wants to devour me.

We ride to a city, ease the bikes down the stairs of a subway clotted with leaves and newspapers, and we leave the garage dimension via a token in a turnstile. Its arms are busted off and the token clinks into the change return for Riley to scoop up, but the whole set up still works as a gateway and the bikes fit through. They fit into the elevator in the next dimension too. Riley opens that gateway with a fire service key and time passes so fast on our side, I don't even see him and Charlie flick through the elevator doors and back again. One second, they're holding their guns, and the next, the weapons are holstered and Riley's telling us it's all clear. *Hopscotching back down the tree then,* my frazzled brain realizes.

The bridge after that is a hotel room door and a mag strip key. Cory holds his breath for that one and mumbles that half the time it doesn't work.

"What do we do then?" I ask numbly.

"Keep trying doors until it does. Sometimes it takes a few different hotels until we hit the right combination."

We luck out five doors in and the big man fist pumps. Riley and Charlie are gone for half an hour. I spend the whole time feeling like a broken little bird under Cory's wing. He seems like a decent guy, I decide. Considerate enough to know when it's time to talk, and when comfortable silence would suit better. The dependable type that people turn to whenever they feel unsteady or lost. The guy that shows up to move furniture when no-one else does. I like him. A desperate part of me wants him to like me too.

Charlie is screaming and dragging Riley draped over her shoulder.

The soldier's right lower leg is gone. Torn off just above the knee. It's all lacerated skin, hamburger gobbets of muscle, and a pink spear of femoral bone. The smell of iron swamps me as arterial blood spurts out of the ragged stump.

They hurtle against the wall opposite the doorway with enough force to rattle the hallway sconces.

"Close it!" Charlie shrieks. "Close the door."

Riley slumps to the ground dropping his pistol and clutching his thigh.

I freeze.

Cory flings the orange pouch down the hall away from us before lunging toward the hotel room door and yanking it closed. Beyond, the ululating howls of maneaters and the crash of glass ricochet in the room. "Ticket?" he bellows. "Tell me you have the ticket, Charlie."

"Oh God," she wails.

He glances over his shoulder, eyes bulging. "Charlie. The ticket!" Something smashes into the door, and the big man grips the lever with both hands and braces.

"I have it," Riley croaks. "Chest pocket."

"David, get it. Show it to me," Cory yells.

Charlie snatches a first aid kit from her bag, tearing a triangular bandage out of its plastic packaging with her teeth.

I slip in the pool of blood forming around Riley, crash to my knees and reach into the zippered pocket of his armored vest.

"Motherfuckers." His breath puffs against my face, fast and shallow. His eyes are wide and white as he stares past his hands at the space where his foot used to be. "Hope I give them indigestion."

Frenzied scratching rips up the carpet at the base of the door, but I barely hear it past the shrill tones filling my head. I find the key card and pull it out, holding it up to Cory.

"Thank Christ," he says. Then to Riley and Charlie, "Anything else left behind?"

"Other than my goddamned leg?" He laughs hysterically.

"Move your hands, Riley," Charlie orders as she threads the

rolled-up bandage under his thigh and then cinches it so tightly that he screams. "I need a tensioner, something strong that I can twist."

"Penlight," Riley slurs, barely clinging to consciousness. "L-left arm pocket."

I pluck the narrow black flashlight from its sleeve in his uniform and hand it to Charlie.

"No. Not yet," Cory barks from his post. Frost creeps up the base of the door. "Don't let him pass out. He's got to eat it first."

"Eat what?" Charlie gapes.

A maneater rams the door hard enough that it sounds like a gunshot cracking down the hallway. We all jump.

"David!" The big man says. "His leg is a keystone until the bastards digest it. They'll find a way to drag our tickets over. They'll use him to do it. We have to break the bridge like you did."

I blink numbly at the blood-smeared keycard still in my hand.

"Jesus Christ, break the ticket!" Cory howls.

I bend the brittle plastic card until it snaps.

A chorus of enraged shrieks blast from the room. Another battering ram strike cracks the doorframe. Doesn't matter that I broke the room key, the maneaters can still hear the siren song of all the other tickets in the orange pouch down the hall, just like I can.

"Now break that half into pieces small enough to swallow." Cory's voice is calmer now, like he's instructing a preschool craft class instead of holding back a tide of death.

"Hurry! He's losing too much blood." Charlie's voice cracks.

My hands are slick as I snap the keycard into smaller shards and pop them into Riley's open mouth like I'm feeding a cracker to a bird.

He winces each time he swallows. When he chokes the fourth piece down, the uproar in the hotel room cuts off like someone clicked a mute button. One second, it sounds like a death metal mosh pit in there, and the next, nothing, like the maneaters just evaporated.

There's only the squeal of the tickets in the pouch down the hall and the three of us heavy breathing with our hearts still thrashing in their cages.

"It worked?" Riley puffs. His skin is the colour of old ashes, his pants soaked in the puddle of red he's sitting in.

Cory grips the door lever like the world will fall apart if he doesn't.

Charlie knots the penlight into the tourniquet and twists it hard enough that Riley shrieks. She doesn't stop when he begs her to, or when he slumps unconscious against the wall. She tightens it until the bleeding stops and then she uses her pulse handgun to cauterize the wound.

It takes everything I've got not to retch at the sizzling sound it makes. Smoke tendrils curl upward from the stump, and the reek of singed flesh sticks in my nostrils.

Cory scoops up Riley's pistol from the carpet and sags to the floor across from the door. "Abort? We taking him down-tree?"

Charlie wipes her nose, hand shaking. "Why're you asking me?"

"You were next in line for primitus this morning, no?"

"How far do you think you could carry him?"

Cory looks down at Riley. "I can carry him as far as you like, but it won't be fast. What the hell happened in there? Damned outdated maps. It wasn't supposed to be rotten."

"Well, it was."

"They pin you in a dark corner?"

She shakes her head and laughs, and it's such a delicate breakable sound so at odds with the roughness of her voice. "You won't believe me."

"Storm?"

"A Goddamned solar eclipse."

"You shitting me?" Cory snorts. "What are the odds?"

"I'm lucky like that."

"How big of a horde?"

"Hard to say. We took the fire exit down and, out of nowhere, the whole back alley just got dark. Looked up and saw the sun blotting out. Then we heard them coming. Couldn't get back fast enough. Riley tried to cover me." She blinks down at him. "We're not going to be able to get him on a motorcycle. Not if he keeps passing out."

Cory rubs his chin. "Your machine's bigger. I could double him on it if we tied him on my back. Or I could try to find something to rig up a trailer, but the whole set up would be a keystone then. We'd be leaving bridges wide open behind us all the way down. Embassy would skin us alive. And if we go on foot, we won't make it before dark. What's the call, boss?"

"I'm not your boss. Don't do that just because you don't want to be the one who catches flak for this."

Adrenalin saps from my bones. This can't be real. Are they actually doing this? Arguing office politics right now?

"Oh, I'm sure they'll drag us both through the coals. Don't you worry about—"

Riley makes a horrible gurgling noise deep in his throat. He vomits and it's startlingly red and foamy.

"Shit." Charlie rolls him onto his side, but he's gasping like a fish out of water now, tendons standing out in his neck as his mouth pops open and closed.

"What's happening?" The words tumble out of my mouth. The ringing in my ears drills in from all sides now.

No-one answers. Cory leans close to Riley's mouth and announces. "Not breathing."

"Shit," she repeats. "Help me get him onto his back."

They pull Riley away from the wall. Blood tracks behind them as they yank the soldier to a dry spot on the carpet. Charlie braces her hands on Riley's chest and starts compressions.

I lose my bearings after that. I think Cory switches out with her a few times when she gets tired, but it gets to a point where she's whimpering as she counts and ignoring the big man every time he calls her name.

"Charlie." He touches her shoulder. "Charlie. Stop. It's time to stop."

She doesn't.

"Charlie." He pulls her away and she howls and bats at his hands before falling back onto her haunches and staring at Riley's face with pinched lips and hard eyes.

A ribbon of blood runs down the corner of his mouth past his slack, grey jaw.

"He's gone, honey," Cory says.

"I babysat him." Her voice cracks.

"I know. Let's find somewhere safe to spend the night, yeah? It's going to get dark soon and we need to set up the lights."

Charlie has crashed on top of a polyester quilt cover. She's sleeping with her boots on. Riley's body lies in the other queen bed, wrapped like a mummy in the sheets. It felt wrong to leave him in the hallway, so we didn't.

I'm lying on a row of couch cushions on the floor with my bandaged leg propped up and throbbing in time with my heart, and Cory's in a fold-out bed far too small for him. He's not sleeping. Over the ringing in my ears, I can hear his breathing, short and uneven.

Banks of LED lights on tripods surround us, bleaching the walls white and highlighting every mote of dust swirling through the room. It takes awhile for me to work up the words, but I eventually spit them out because I know Cory won't dodge the question like Charlie might. "What happened to him?" I ask into the stale electric air.

"Hmm?" Springs creak and Cory tips the corner of his sleep mask up.

"Riley, he puked blood at the end." I leave my question hanging and when the big man doesn't answer, I ask outright "Why would he puke blood if only his leg was hurt?"

"Wasn't his leg that did that, kid." He sniffs. "I imagine it was the ticket shards. People have tried swallowing the things whole in the past and it tends to end with a dark walker tearing them wide open or massive unexplained internal bleeding. Whatever tickets are made from, it doesn't seem to be compatible with most folk's insides. I was hoping a broken ticket would be survivable for him, like it was for you." He turns to me, squinting past the blinding lights. "You do anything special when you swallowed yours?"

"I-I don't think so." I take several breaths before asking a question that's been needling me for hours. "What did you mean when you said the maneat—dark walkers would use Riley to pull tickets over?"

He pinches the bridge of his nose and stares up at the ceiling. "They can't come through gateways without a ticket, but they can reach. They can influence. There's been documented cases of gatekeepers—who damned well know better—going into trances, just opening up gates and handing a horde a ticket, not even crying out while they get eaten alive."

My mind flashes back to James sleepwalking, standing zoned-out in front of the cottage door while that macabre black hand reached for his ankle. How I zombie-walked into an infested world after convincing my family to leave and then I fell asleep in a lawn chair at the beach with the Pithos key stuck in the door on the wrong side with me. "Jesus Christ," I whisper. "We going back in the morning?"

"Down-tree? Not likely now. No point. Riley's dead, and you're priority number one anyhow. Whole point of this mission is getting your strength back. Embassy won't want us back in Prime unless you're healthy. If they saw you the shade of white you are right now, I'd wager they'd just turn us around and send us back up here. Don't worry. Only one more jump, and we've got alternate tickets and routes for emergencies like this. We'll have you right as rain in no time."

I want to believe him. I want to be strong and steady like he is, but I don't think that's going to happen. I don't think I'll ever be right again.

We leave Riley behind in the hotel bed when we go. We leave his motorcycle too, parked out front. I don't know how to ride it, and we don't have to worry about it being a keystone when we leave. Riley was our primitus, our inadvertent mule. As soon as he died, all his bridges collapsed. And all of us—including everything we brought—became incorporated into this world. We're not connected to any gateways, but we can't stay here. According to Charlie it's not far enough up-tree for me to convalesce. A nasty headache, fresh fever, and redoubled swelling of my infected leg suggest she's right.

It seems incredibly callous abandoning Riley, but we can't take the soldier's body with us, and from the way Charlie and Cory are acting, they're either both exceptionally desensitized or Prime just doesn't adhere to the same funerary customs as the world I grew up in. Neither of them seem sentimental about Riley's remains. They don't even talk about burying or cremating him. Makes sense, I guess, if your whole world grew up mired in a generational war that's swallowed up your casualties while they were half a universe away. I don't imagine many bodies get shipped home to Prime for their last rites, not if their primitus died.

Every light lit. Nothing left behind. Except Riley.

After a quick detour around the infected hotel world, we reach our last gateway late the next morning—the one that opens into the dimension parallel to my family's offshoot world.

It's a church. Its ticket is a crucifix. I don't know if Charlie and Cory are just unnerved, but the prep is different this time. Charlie takes out her LED light backpack and headlamp and hooks them up to her power supply before donning them. Cory takes out a large knife and he hands another to me. "No surprises this time. This world's a charted rotten branch. Infected. So, look alive, just in case," he says before gripping my shoulder. "You're not going to drop on me, are you, kid?"

"Nothing's going to come through." Charlie loops the crucifix around her neck, and hands the orange bag to Cory. "I'll make sure it's clear. We do a bit of work and then we come back here where it's safe. Rinse and repeat tomorrow. And the next day, until you're healthier. All good, right David?"

"Yeah. All Good," I lie. I can't stop my voice from shaking.

"What did you do?" She fires a hard glance at Cory.

"Me? Jesus, he's just rattled. Can you blame him?"

"This is more than that. What did you tell him?"

"I answer him when he asks questions, that's all. We're not all brick walls, Charlie. You never even fucking told me he was from an offshoot."

"It was classified," she barks.

"I'm fine," I insist, suddenly desperate to impress them both.

I'm not. Of course, I'm not. I watched a man die while everyone else acted like it was just another day at work. My clothes are still stained with his blood. I'm a relic in the world I was born in, and I've been erased in the one I grew up in. My biological parents are dust, and my real ones haven't even had time to miss me yet. We're going to a dimension parallel to James, but we may as well be cars whipping past each other on a cosmic highway. *I'll never see him again.* I realize. *I'll never know if he's okay. If any of them are.*

I can't accept that. I just can't.

Chapter Eight

The Embassy plan works. Days into our two-week shift, my energy returns, and my leg infection clears up. I can walk reasonable distances without feeling like a bag of shit, which is good, because, as it turns out, our job consists of a lot of walking. We're mostly tracking, collecting, and destroying keystones. Dead keystones—one's who's carrier has expired—just become a part of the world they're in. Once the bridge they reinforced collapses, any object alien to the dimension they're in aren't keystones anymore.

Live keystones however, one's still holding open bridges, they resonate differently than the foreign worlds they're in. They're beacons. I can't hear them like I can the tickets, but the Embassy has engineered equipment capable of tracking them. Compared to what we've been through to get here, it initially sounds like a cake walk. How hard could it be, wandering around on sunny days like scavengers with a metal detector on a beach, picking up the baubles we find and destroying them?

Here's the thing though.

Maneaters don't just track tickets. They hunt live keystones too and they swallow any they find in a concerted effort to keep bridges open so they can *influence* tickets toward them and expand into uneaten dimensions. Lucky for us, this branch is a recently stripped one. The hordes here are small ones, still bloated, slow, and mostly uninterested in us. During daylight hours, they den up wherever they can find suitable darkness.

Cory tracks ones who have swallowed keystones. Most days we're not treasure hunting. We're actually hunting. This involves my chaperones leaving my fragile ass in a secure, well-lit area at high noon to go persuade a dark walker out of its hibernaculum. They use alternate tickets from the orange pouch as bait. Nothing else would lure a well sated creature into the sunlight. Then they stun it with a pulsed laser shot to the face and take it 'offline' with a rod through an ocular cavity to penetrate and destroy its brain stalk.

Cory's words, not mine. I've never been there for the killing blow, thank Christ. It's harrowing enough dealing with the dead ones.

The first day that Cory and Charlie haul a flaccid maneater toward me on a makeshift sled, adrenaline pumps through me so intensely, I puke. It isn't just the raw memory of what the wretched things did to Riley, or them coming for me as I swallowed the broken Pithos key. I'm not squeamish about the dead body either because it doesn't feel like looking at something dead, not like how it felt with Riley. More like watching a massive predator behind glass at a zoo. Fascination, fear, and horror all warring in your belly at the same time. The certainty that this is something *built* to kill you, and it's mere inches away, separated from you by the flimsiest of barriers.

I've gotten better about the puking since then—good thing because we wear face-shields and filter masks during necroscopies. I can't imagine how messy vomiting in this get-up would be. But I'm still keyed-up and unnerved the entire time we're dissecting. I don't think that'll get better with time. You've got to be a special type to do this for a living. And I'm not it.

Cory is.

Today, we're in a mechanic's shop. The big man chose the building because it has a rail-mounted crane on the ceiling and bays with glass garage doors that let in plentiful light. Mechanical lifting devices help. Maneater bodies are heavy and awkward to move without them. The creature before this one was so huge, we had to dissect it where it fell in the street. Not ideal. Especially with its live brethren still ricocheting around inside the windowless casino they were holed up in, tipping over slot machines and blasting us with ear-shattering screeches and icy wafts of air.

Those screams. They sounded like words. Nothing I understood, but not incoherent babble either.

I've been having trouble sleeping since Riley. And when I do drift off, most nights I dream about James and wake up aching for a family that was never mine. I'm settling into that fact now, as much as it hurts.

Our current specimen is laid out on its side on two tool benches we pushed together. Its neck, forelimbs and rear limbs are all ratchet strapped down to the table legs, not only to keep them out of the way, but also because no-one has found a reliable indicator of death for the ghastly creatures. There have been cases of catalogers being killed by dark walkers they presumed dead, that inexplicably revived and attacked mid-dissection.

"Those idiots cut corners on restraining their cadavers properly and they didn't open the skull case to verify the brain stalk was fully destroyed." Cory huffed when he told me. "Always tie the buggers down like you expect them to wake up halfway through, and always open up the skull first to verify, and you'll be fine."

I can't express how *not* comforting that piece of knowledge is. And no matter how well restrained they are, I can't get used to being up close to the malicious aliens, never mind methodically butchering them. It's not just the pallid, patchwork skin bristling with hair, the skull-like face, or the antler appendages twisting out of their spines. It's the cold.

Maneaters run at a far lower body temperature than sapiens.

I'm up to my wrists in blood and I'm freezing. My hands throb like I've been reaching into an ice-fishing hole that's slushing over. The long rubber gloves Cory provided are insulated, but they aren't helping much. Every time I reach into the body cavity to remove an organ as instructed my fingers go numb. It doesn't help that the thing's claws occasionally click like morse code on the metal tabletop. Grey muscles keep spasming, and the cut-out section of ribcage on the floor twitches even now, hours into the procedure. My mentor says electrical activity persists for days at which point the dead body's temperature rises to ambient, triggering rapid decomposition.

"They don't come back from that," he assures me.

Right now, he's elbow deep in the large intestine of the creature on the table while I'm hauling out the liver he just snipped free. Condensation forms and rolls off it as mist while I hoist the chilled organ into warmer air.

"Watch it!" he snaps, nodding toward the exposed rib ends. "Those gloves aren't puncture proof and the rib shears leave bone shards sharp enough to cut you. We've got no idea what kind of nasty microbes these bastards are teaming with. I told you earlier why I was precutting a loose flap of thoracic skin. Were you even listening? Weigh that organ then drape the skin back in place over the rib ends before you hurt yourself."

I listen. I already know that my teacher is all business when it comes to work. No laughing or chuckling. It's like he just switches his personality off. I know he prefers to open a thorax with rib shears as opposed to an electric saw because they're faster, don't need a power source, and won't cause overspray issues. See all the new things I'm picking up in Cory's Accelerated Education Program for Mostly Useless Assistants? It's easier to memorize small facts because the big concepts are still eating me alive whenever I consider them.

My face shield fogs up as I set the liver on the hanging scale, wipe off my gloved hands on a towel, and awkwardly write the weight down in the spiral bound notebook. My fingers feel like ice cubes and my writing looks like a five-year-old's. I'll be sure to hear about tidiness in record-keeping later. Taking the purple, many-lobed organ off the scale tray, I set it on the plastic wrapped table next to the jellied remains of the brain stalk, the stomach, two creepy-as-hell still-beating hearts, and three sets of air sacs. Then I return to the maneater and drape the excess skin Cory left behind over its quivering ribcage.

"I don't get it," I say, watching him press aside a loop of bowels to reach the secondary gastric crop. It's one of the spots that maneaters store non-digestibles.

"Get what?" Cory clamps off the large intestine.

"Keystone mules. Why kill people when your population is already so low? Why not send a ticket through a gate another way? Remote control device or a trained lab rat or something?" It's off topic, but when we're eviscerating something, I find I prefer to talk about anything else other than the task at hand, and Cory is a lot more open with his answers than Charlie. She doesn't stick around for the dissections.

He snorts. "You think that if taping a ticket to a bloody mouse and shooing it through a gateway was the solution, the Embassy wouldn't have tried it a hundred times by now? Naw, it has to be something sentient. Something smart. Primates worked, but we ran out of those pretty quickly. Dark walkers only kill sentient creatures too. Apes, dogs, whales, octopus. You ever notice that? They leave everything else behind."

"Why?"

"Your guess is as good as mine. The religious zealots would have you believe only smart stuff has souls, and we're being punished for something. Hand me those tweezers."

I do as I'm told, and Cory grips an ulcerous growth, snips it off, and hands the pincers back to me. "Get that on a slide, please," he says.

I shave a thin slice off the tumour and lay it on a glass slide. Then

I place a cover slip on top, add a drop of staining solution at one end and watch the sample pull dye across it. I wipe off the excess solution with a towel, like Cory taught me, and I label the slide with a marker. "There's something else I don't get."

"Yeah?" Cory says distractedly.

"Everett visited the same worlds before me. He left notes." We'd spoken of Everett already.

"Smart guy. He left you a bread crumb trail."

"How? None of the changes *I* made stuck. The worlds reset each time." I remembered shattering every one of my mother's dishes in a rage, over and over again, closing the door on a floor crunchy with fangs of broken glass, and re-opening it to all of the tableware intact, back in the cupboards, ready to smash again. Childish. What I wouldn't give to hold her now.

"Think of it like a bus stop. The first gatekeepers had the ability to manufacture and aim a ticket wherever and whenever they liked. But we can't. Near as we can figure, those original routes imprinted on the tickets. That energy surge that accompanied the Breach, it fried lots of tickets. The ones that are still functioning, they're locked onto routes now. They just take the same path, over and over. Changes you make in a world don't set in until the next loop through. Your Everett, he'd have never seen the notes he left until he repeated the circuit."

My throat dries out. "112 worlds," I say quietly. Everett had written 112 different dates in the dictionary. A pattern that repeated after it reached the end of the list. 112 different dimensions.

"112? Christ, that's the longest bus route I've ever heard of. Your guy was dedicated."

"He was." I clear my throat to cover the emotion in those words. After several breaths, I say. "One more question."

"I'm all ears. Help me lift this. It's distended."

I hold onto the swollen gastric crop while Cory clamps it and cuts it away from where it attaches to the intestines. "When a bridge is opened but no keystone is in place, it's a patchy connection, right?"

"I told you as much."

"So, when it does connect, anyone could get through it, right? Even without a ticket? Couldn't a maneater do the same? Just cross the bridge while it was connected? Why do they always need a ticket, but sometimes we don't?"

"They don't all need a ticket, just one in a horde does. A group of them is a superorganism. More like one being than many. If one of them had snatched the keycard back there in the hotel room hallway, the whole horde would have breached, however many were in range."

They communicate via sound and radio signals. The appendages on their backs are organic antenna. Cory told me that too. Idly, I wonder just how many aliens this man has methodically butchered and catalogued. "But one of them needs a ticket," I confirm. "They can't cross a connected bridge without it?"

"They can't." He confirms, injecting a single drop of liquid from a syringe into the creature's cracked open skull. Odd. It's clear. Doesn't look like staining solution.

"Why?"

He shrugs. "Our ancestors came up with ticket technology, so I imagine the whole thing was engineered with humanoids in mind, or at least sentients from the same universal tree. Dark walkers hopped over from an entirely different tree. Look at 'em. They're built different than us. Bloody genetic chimeras. Dozens of different sets of DNA in every one of them. Did you know that? Bunch of lifeforms all mashed into one. Be damned glad they need tickets, or they'd have already spread a hell of a lot faster than they have, and we'd have been little more than shit stains on the carpet as soon as Riley opened up that hotel room door. Alright, let's see what we've got."

He takes the bloated crop to the table and uses a scalpel to slice it open. Several objects spill out. A pair of dentures, some loose change, a driver's license with writing in a language I don't recognize, and a small rectangular tin. There seems to be a critical mass that makes something big enough to be a keystone. Cory's never found something smaller than a centimeter. He figures it's because the smaller the object is, the smaller its resonant signature.

"At some point, the mass is just too small to hold a gateway open," he'd told me yesterday as we inspected all our equipment before crossing over the bridge for the night. "Good thing too or every damned pebble caught in the treads of these bike tires would turn into a keystone." Then he flicked out the pebbles anyways, just to be safe.

I line the items up in a row on the top edge of the table. Charlie will scan them with the keystone detector when she gets back to see which ones are the live ones that led her to this dark walker. The false teeth and the ID will burn easily enough in a regular fire, but if the coins and the tin are live, she'll have to use a concentrator on her handgun to vaporize them. Her weapon only fires so many bursts before it needs to be charged with more power than we've brought, so she's careful to preserve her shots. No need to waste energy vaporizing a keystone that's already deactivated.

When I flip the tin over, the top side is rusted, but still stamped with embossed lettering. It's not a lozenge tin, like I initially thought.

It's a tobacco tin.

My stomach pinches and my mouth dries out. *Oh God. Everett.*

We finish the rest of the necroscopy mostly in silence. We take warm up breaks when our fingers lose dexterity. Then Cory methodically cuts up every organ and takes samples of it. He can't bring slides home with maneater tissue on them, but he'll take multiple high magnification photos of them and catalogue them all before the samples degrade. Then I'll sanitize all the slides and tools, checking our inventory lists to make sure everything is accounted for. It wouldn't do to leave something behind in a dead maneater. It's a methodical and meticulous procedure, and the whole time I'm doing it, I can't stop glancing over at the little tin on the table.

It could be his. What are the chances there are two tobacco tin keystones? It could be Everett's.

Charlie returns from her outing with a keystone that hasn't yet been discovered by the maneaters in this dimension, a wristwatch she found in a creek bed. When she scans the items on our table, the dentures are the only live keystone in our bunch. We burn them before we leave for the day.

And that's when I do the dumbest thing I've ever done in my life. I don't leave the tobacco tin behind with the other dead keystones. I pocket it while Cory and Charlie aren't looking. I know it's incredibly stupid and dangerous to bring it back to the safe world we're spending the night in. Doing so will turn it into a new live keystone. But the tin is from *my* world, I'm sure of it. It's something Everett held once. The only tie I have to the home I left behind and to the man I never met who inadvertently got tangled up in dimensions, just like I have. Everett left notes. He didn't even know me, and he helped me. He died trying to set things right when he lost this tin. It feels sacred, like the little envelope of fingernails kamikaze pilots left behind so their families would have a piece of them when they held a funeral. I can't let this piece of Everett go. I just can't. Besides, I can put it back on its proper side in two days and no-one will know the difference. The crucifix ticket runs an incredibly short bus route. It only skips to two other dimensions before repeating. Cory confirmed it today. I wasn't sure of it at the time, but we've already seen changes we've made showing up in the next loop. We've had to haul a severely decomposing maneater off the garage tables once already. Now I know it was the same one we dissected three days ago. That means I can hold tight to the tobacco tin for a little bit, put it back in a few days and no-one will be the wiser. It won't hurt anybody.

Chapter Nine

I'm standing in front of James again. He's leaving for trade school, scuffing his feet behind that shitty Ford Tempo of his, overstuffed duffle bag on the ground between us. Tears prick my eyes as I stare at the birthday present he made for me, a project he'd made for school. A survival kit. He's holding it out right now, a lumpy package swathed in newspaper. It looks like he hired someone with no thumbs to wrap it. Long, dog-eared flaps of Scotch tape stitch together puckering seams.

I don't care if this is a dream, I'm so overwhelmed at the sight of him, the easy confidence in his voice, how he calls me Skippy like he has for as long as I can remember, I can't stop smiling. I can hardly follow the conversation. God, I needed this tonight.

I open the gift and pore over each of the items inside. A compass, fishing line and hooks, a fire-starting flint, a condom. I snort laugh at that, and my big brother reaches out and musses my hair. As he does, I notice his left pant leg is torn and three ugly, half-healed lacerations rake across his bare ankle. My breath hangs up in my chest.

His injury. It's healing.

Something prods my hip bone. I reach down and feel Everett's tobacco tin still snug in my jeans pocket.

The road liquifies under my feet. Literally. *Oh my God. There was no ankle wound when I dreamed about this before. I'm holding the damned tin. This isn't a dream.* I lock gazes with James, and I see it in his eyes, this odd, incongruent hope, like he knows too and he's hoping I'll tell him he's right. *If it's not a dream, he shouldn't be able to see me. I'm not synced to this dimension. This is impossible.* But it's happening. This is real. He sees me.

"Thanks, James," I say, and the pavement sucks me under. *No, Oh God.* I can feel it rolling over my hips, crushing my abdomen, coiling around my chest like a massive conglomerate snake. I've fallen into hot, setting cement and now there's gravel and tar lapping at my neck, scraping against my tightly pressed lips, cramming into my ears. *Help. Help me. Oh Jesus, please.* But I'm drowning in darkness. It's pressing so hard into me, it's seeping into my pores, black, smug and certain of my death. It's so much stronger than I am. I don't stand a chance. It steamrolls me.

I can't move. I'm buried alive. My body is screaming for air while my limbs petrify in the solidifying pavement. Just when I think the blackness is going to kill me. I fall through the other side.

Someone is shaking me hard, but I don't care because I'm out of the darkness and I'm breathing. Blood thunders between my ears. I claw at the person gripping me like a drowning casualty clinging to a lifeguard, but they lean into me, their forearm cutting across my windpipe. Suddenly, I'm not breathing again.

"What did you do?" Cory bellows. He's holding a surgical knife inches from my face. "What the *fuck* did you just do?"

"Don't kill him." LED lights blaze above me. Charlie silhouette is limned with light. She's aiming her gun at Cory's head. I'm in the pastor's residence behind the church gateway, not with James. Not home. "Cory, don't kill him," Charlie repeats.

"The little fucker blipped." There's no warmth in his voice at all. No hint of the tenuous comradery I've been trying to build between us.

Starbursts bloom in my vision.

"You're choking him."

"I'll do more than that. He *blipped* Charlie. I saw it. Look out the window." He nods towards the glass. A sickle moon hangs like a clipped fingernail in the darkness. "The bastard opened a gate to somewhere in the *middle of the night*. Check your tickets. Now."

My eyes are going to explode. I'm jacked on adrenalin, but nowhere near as strong as the man strangling me.

"Let him breathe first."

Cory eases his arm off enough for me to suck in several choppy breaths, but he presses the point of his blade against my cheek. "Embassy wants you back alive, but I'm pretty sure I'll only get a slap on the wrist if I mutilate you, so how about we talk about where you just went."

"Home," I choke. "My world."

"Bullshit." Flecks of spit rain onto my hot cheeks. Cory's eyes bulge. "We don't have a ticket to your safe world."

"I'm not missing any," Charlie announces, orange zippered bag in hand.

"What?" Cory turns to her.

"They're all here. I'm not missing any tickets. Let him up. He didn't go anywhere."

"He did! I saw it, Charlie. I was up. It's my shift. I was watching you sleeping beauties, cursing out how loud you both snore when he blipped. His sleeping bag deflated. Thirty seconds later, he's back, lying on top of it." He hisses to me, "You've smuggled a ticket with you from Prime then, haven't you?"

"No," I gulp, chest aching not just from the panic, but from the sinking feeling that Cory thinks I'd knowingly betray him.

"Where the hell would he get a ticket, Cory?" Charlie says. "I was supervising him the whole time. The only time I wasn't, he was in the apartment with you."

"Not a ticket. In ... my pocket." I point towards my jeans.

"Take it out," Cory demands.

With shuddering hands, I wiggle the tobacco tin out of my front pocket and hold it up.

He snatches it, frowning. "This … this is from the maneater today. The keystone. You took it?"

"Yeah."

"Why in the hell would you—you know what? Doesn't matter."

"Shit." Charlie lowers her gun and scrambles through the orange bag until she finds the crucifix.

"You better keep an iron grip on that," Cory says. "They're going to do everything they can to lure it over now." He scowls, knife still pressed to my cheek. "Goddamnit, I was sure the tin was a keystone, not a ticket. It was in the secondary crop."

Maneaters have two internal pouches, one attached to their intestines for keystones and one in their throat for tickets, so they can regurgitate them to use as needed. I know the tobacco tin isn't a ticket. I'd hear it if it was, and the only ringing noise is the aggravating tones from the orange bag Charlie's holding.

"It's not a ticket," she says slowly.

"Please don't cut me," I add.

"There's a gate already open then, that we didn't know about?" Cory asks her.

"Not a gate. You didn't see him go through a gateway, did you?"

The knife trembles before the big man pulls away from me and leans back. "Naw … oh shit. He just blipped."

"Without going through a gate." Charlie sounds scared shitless. I look over to her from where I'm lying on the floor, breathing like I just collapsed at the finish line of a race.

"That … that's impossible," he says.

She holsters her weapon, crouches down beside Cory and puts a hand on his arm. "Are you sure that's what you saw? I mean, we're tired. We've all been working hard. Maybe—"

"Don't patronize me." The big man shakes her off. "I'm not tired, and I know what I fucking saw. He didn't move. He was there, and then he was gone and back again." He points the knife toward me again. "Where did you go?"

I sit up slowly, hands shaking, teeth chattering. I think I'm going into shock. "I went home."

"He's lying, Charlie. No way he went that far." Cory insists. "His home is an offshoot. The time dilation is too much. If he went there, even for half a second, he'd have been gone a hell of a lot longer from here. And he wasn't. Only thirty seconds. I fucking counted. I started yelling at you to wake up and he was back."

"I went home," I repeat loudly.

"How?" Charlie presses. She puts her warm hand over mine and uses the soft voice she employed when I was bleeding out at the cottage, the one that means shit is serious but we're pretending it isn't so we can get through it. "This is important, Sunshine."

"I don't know."

"For fuck sakes." Cory runs his hands through his hair.

"Pack up," Charlie orders him curtly. "Give me the tin and I'll vaporize it. Mission's aborted. Directive has changed. We're going back to Prime first thing in the morning."

"Can we talk about this?" I can't sleep. Near death experiences do that to you, I guess. Cory is splayed on the couch, long limbs hanging off the arm rests. His eyelids flutter and his mouth hangs open. Drool trickles into his beard. If he's feigning sleep, he's doing a hell of a job of it.

Charlie is restless. Hours after I woke everyone, she took the tobacco tin from me and went into the other room to destroy it. She's still pacing, fidgeting with her pearl earrings, building static between us that I'd very much like to discharge safely. "I'm not lying to you."

"I know."

"Whatever I did, it wasn't on purpose. I was sleeping. I don't even know how I did it."

"I believe you," she says without looking at me.

"No-one's ever done that before?"

A frantic laugh escapes her that makes Cory stir in his sleep. "Interdimensional travel without a ticket or a gateway? One that circumvents time dilation? No, David. No-one's ever done that before."

I nod, lick my lips. The image of red, foamy blood erupting from Riley's mouth overcomes me. It flares up at the oddest times. "Hey, did they ever find the piece I swallowed? All those scans. All the IDOCS sessions. They wanted that broken ticket so bad, and Prime has the technology to surgically implant light shows under people's skin. I kind of assumed taking out a key would be a breeze."

She stops pacing and blinks up at the ceiling. "They never found it. You never passed it. The doctors figured you absorbed it somehow."

"Oh," I say. Nothing else. Not *'Oh, that's mildly terrifying'* or *'Oh, that's got to screw with a guy's insides.'* Just. Oh.

She starts her circuit around the room again.

"Charlie?" I croak.

"Yeah?"

"If you take me back there, I'll never see the outside of a hamster ball again. I'll be their guinea pig forever."

"Yeah." She bites her lip and keeps walking.

I blink rapidly against the stinging in my eyes. *Come on. Say something smart. Convince her.* "Don't. Please. Don't take me back there."

Her voice shakes when she answers. "Go to sleep, David."

We go back the same way we came. When we stop at the hotel where we slept that first awful night, Riley's body is gone. The room has been torn apart by predators. Not maneaters. Something from here.

There're slender, dog-like paw prints leading into the hotel from an open door in the fire exit stairwell.

We carry on in silence to the elevator gateway, the subway, and finally, the grocery store. Charlie doesn't speak to me the whole way down, and Cory's reverted to cold, all-business mode. I feel invisible again, and I should be used to it, but I can't stand it with them, can't stomach the idea that I thought I was making progress, coming out of my shell and building meaningful connections, when in fact, Charlie and Cory only ever saw me as a job. A mission. And now, I'm an aborted mission.

There are no wait times on the way down the tree except going into the elevator world. Charlie and Cory walk the bikes back into the shipping bay office. She grabs the shopping cart we left, plunks the token into it, and crosses the threshold with the broken sliding door. Then, she immediately re-appears and waves us in.

The big man's been quiet the entire time. He nods and hands her the orange bag and we all enter the store and exit into its mirror parking lot. He cinches his hat down and walks out onto the broken tarmac ahead of us.

This is it. One short walk, and I'll be back in a room full of military guys with guns. This is probably the last day I'll ever be outside. My mind feels soupy, soaked in anxiety. My body's operating on autopilot, plunking one foot ahead of the other.

Charlie grabs my wrist hard enough to make me wince. She pulls me to a stop in front of the door with the faded banana poster. That's when I notice that she's white-knuckling the shopping cart handle bar.

Cory turns around when he doesn't hear wheels rattling behind him. Broken asphalt crunches under his shoes. "What's up?" he says.

Charlie draws her weapon. "Go home, Cory."

His shoulders slump. "No. Nope. We're not doing this."

She lets go of me, fishes out the Toyota keys, and tosses them. Cory doesn't catch them. They land inches away from his shoes.

"Go home to Lee and tell them you didn't play any part in this."

His voice is low. Reasonable. Terrified. "Charlie, I *didn't* play any part in this. Don't do this. They know you've been going back there. They *will* hunt you down. And we both know they won't show any mercy when they find you."

We all stand there. Static. Charlie's breathing in zen mode, her gun aimed and steady. Cory's holding his duffle bag like someone abandoned him at a train station, a laser bead jittering on his chest. Then the big man moves toward us.

She shoots him in the upper arm. The blast torques him sideways. His bag tumbles out of his grip, and smoke curls from the singed hole in his jacket before he clamps his hand over it.

"Fuck! Charlie!"

"Go home," she barks. Then she corrals me toward the door with the grocery cart. We blip onto the other side, and she marches toward the cart corral, gun still out.

"What did you do?" I yelp. "Jesus, he can still come through. You shot him."

She answers without looking back. "It's already been fifteen minutes on his side. If he was going to come over, he'd already be here." She slams the cart in line with her duffle bag still in it, plugs in the key and pulls out her token. "Come on."

"Where are we going?"

She shrugs off her jacket, tears into the sleeve's inseam, and yanks out a coin, slotting it into the cart she just locked. It's a ticket. I can hear it. "Somewhere better than a hamster ball with an IDOCS up your asshole. How's that sound?"

"Really compelling actually."

She slaps the orange bag with all the other tickets against my chest. "Hold this and wait for the all-clear." And then she pushes the shopping cart toward the broken sliding door.

I kind of want to puke.

I kind of want to kiss her.

Chapter Ten

We push through the entrance of the grocery store and out into a freshly paved parking lot full of clean cars. It's hotter and thick with humidity compared to the dimension we just left, but that's not what throws me.

It's populated.

Charlie takes one hand off the cart to grab me by the wrist and U-turn me toward the exit door. I nearly collide with a little old man wearing a neat grey moustache and a huge set of sunglasses that fit over his prescription lenses. He's carrying a flower bouquet and a twenty-pound bag of potatoes. I twist aside and squash against the edge of the sliding door to avoid bowling him over, but the guy doesn't even turn his head to acknowledge me. "There are people here," I wheeze.

No shit, Sherlock.

Charlie still has her gun drawn. The weapon is conspicuous enough that it'd be hard to miss, but none of the folks laden with groceries notice it, and they don't see us either. "Course there's people," she says. "Wouldn't be much worth saving if every dimension was abandoned now, would there?"

I follow her into the store, uncertain in my invisibility. Even though I've lived most my life cloaked in insignificance, in an unfamiliar world it feels like trespassing, like I could be exposed at any moment.

Charlie makes a beeline for the candy aisle and throws three boxes of Hot Tamales into the cart on top of her duffle bag. Then she heads for the exit.

I'm still digesting the imagery of Cory's smoking arm, the pain twisting his face, and the steel in Charlie's voice as we skirt around a docile line up of carts and shoppers with loyalty cards already in hand. My mind's still grinding gears as we burst back out into the sunlight and Charlie slaps an arm across my chest before I step off the curb.

A car barrels by inches from my toes. The driver doesn't swerve or touch the brakes.

"David! Careful. Dimensions know when we don't belong, and they erase us if they can. Don't make it easy."

"Sorry," I mumble.

We cross the lot, return the cart, and collect the coin—a ticket I'm assuming Charlie didn't obtain legally if she concealed it by sewing it into her jacket. She slips it into the orange bag then shoulders her duffle bag and marches down the street to a bus stop.

"Hey, what are we doing?" I ask as I trot after her. Honest to God, I really am a damned puppy. "You kind of lost me at the undermine-your-partner-and-flee part."

She holsters her gun, glances back at the grocery store. "You just showed us that you can do something else the Embassy's never seen before—blip to another world without using a gateway or a ticket, and you had two witnesses, who are consequently duty bound to take you back so that the scientists back at Prime can peel back all your layers and see what makes you tick. Cory has Lee to worry about. I'm not tied down like he is. What we're doing is hiding you up-tree. There are more dimensional branches up here than further down. More hideouts. Hopefully, we can pass enough time for the Embassy to cool their jets. You stay up-tree long enough and everyone that's pissed at you either retires or dies. And maybe you don't become a science experiment for the rest of your life."

"Not your first time pissing off people enough that they take decades to cool down?"

She smiles. All gums and bright teeth.

My stupid stomach flips and I think *Oh God, I'll do whatever she asks if she keeps smiling like that.*

"Not my first time," she confirms.

I clear my throat. "Cory said *'they know you've been going back there.'* 'They' as in the Embassy? They've caught you here before?"

She sobers.

 "This is your safe world, isn't it?"

"It is." She rocks onto her tiptoes, searching down the street.

"We can't stay here if the Embassy knows it's your hide out."

"Do you think I'm stupid?"

"No—Jesus. Charlie, I didn't mean... I'm kind of flailing here. Throw me a rope, will you? You just shot a guy I thought you were pals with. I'm having trouble keeping up is all."

A diesel Greyhound bus rumbles toward us and she relaxes at the sight of it. "We're not staying here. I've got a fresh ticket to another dimension the Embassy hasn't got its claws in yet. We just need to make a stop first. Fair enough?"

"Okay," I say, like she's actually waiting for my permission.

The bus is congested. Too many people breathing too close together. We stand, because if we sit, we'd risk being crushed by fellow riders who can't see us. I get wedged in behind this old woman with a pleated polyester skirt, a tight perm, and a severe flatulence problem. The windows are closed. It's sweltering and everyone is doing their best to ignore the fact that this grandma is barefacedly dropping bombs on us all. Not exactly how I pictured my daring escape.

We transfer twice. Traffic thins, thoroughfares melt into suburbia parceled into bland yards, severely trimmed hedges and wholesome

American dream homes. Charlie leads me to a bungalow with peeling white paint and chipped black shutters. A huge lilac tree dominates the front yard, flowers spent and drooping on its limbs like melted cotton candy. It's crawling with bees and wasps. Charlie pushes past a wood-framed screen door and into a front entry, beckoning me to follow.

I deke around a trim woman with a smart pixie cut, oversized denim shirt and cargo shorts. "What is wrong with this door? Gene?" she says. "I think the latch is broken again. Every damned mosquito in the neighborhood is going to be in here, I know it." She closes the door behind us and straightens the plethora of shoes piled on the welcome mat in the front entry.

Charlie's already turning down a long hallway. I glimpse a living room with an overstuffed sectional, a half-finished puzzle on the table, and Hot Wheels racetracks strewn all over the carpet. Attached is a sleek kitchen with a clock that reads 8:00.

"Come on," Charlie whispers.

We pad down a dark hallway filled with hand-crafted wooden signs with inspirational sayings. I'm just passing one with chunky cursive that states: *Falling down is an accident. Staying down is a choice* when Charlie swerves left into a bedroom.

It's a kid's room. A boy's, I think, judging from the pair of inside out sweatpants on the floor with boxer shorts still attached. The movie posters on the wall are tattered, shredded renditions of some super-hero in orange tights who I don't recognize. He's standing before the silhouette of a wicked looking fighter plane, glaring skyward like a bird just crapped on his jet. A bunk bed dominates one corner of the room with a tightly made lower bed and a mess of twisted blankets on the upper level. Beside it, thumbtacked to the roof on strands of fishing line are dozens of bright, patterned origami cranes.

Charlie rakes her hand through the flock gently, setting all the paper birds to wobbling. Pulling one of the boxes of candy out of her duffle, she traces a finger over the white lettering. Then, she sets it down on a nightstand already crowded with five water bottles and a framed photo amidst several fruit snack wrappers. She adjusts the box of Hot Tamales several times, like it's a precious museum exhibit. She picks up the tarnished silver frame and wipes the dust off its glass. On the right side of the photo is a blond kid—maybe eight years old—with a bowl cut, a striped shirt, and skinned knees. He's pale, freckled, clasping hands with someone younger than him in a yellow sun dress. A toddler maybe, I can't tell, because that side of the picture is so water damaged it's just a blur. Only the side of the dress and one pudgy dark brown hand remains unscathed.

Dark brown skin. It hits me as Charlie clenches her jaw and slows down her breathing.

"That you?" I whisper and she jumps.

"Yeah," she finally croaks. "It's the only picture left. The basement flooded and Mom—I mean Samantha—kept all the family albums down there." She wipes her thumb over the muddied image. "Some of the pictures made it out okay. None of mine though. I checked. Worlds erase you when you don't belong. You know how it is."

"I do." My family forgot me before I even left. My world was ruthlessly efficient at erasing me, even while I was still in it. *So, why do I want to go back so badly?* I feel like I've swallowed something dry and hastily chewed. *Same reason as Charlie does. We still love them even if they don't remember us.* Our connections, our bridges, they're one-sided, but they're all that's anchoring us in the messy swirl of dimensions around us. My fingers ache to reach out and take Charlie's hand in mine, but I'm pretty sure she'd deck me—maybe even shoot me—if I did. You don't touch skittish people with guns. "Your brother's room?"

"Ours." She squints at the immaculately-made bottom bunk. "We shared it. His name's Adam." Her face crumples as she looks back down at the picture, and I turn away.

I pretend to examine the ratty posters while she places the photo gently back in place and re-adjusts the box of Hot Tamales.

"When I was really little, he gave me one of these. I guess I thought it was a jellybean. The cinnamon burned my mouth so bad that I spit it out. Adam thought it was hilarious. After that, it was this weird competition between us. We'd save up loose change, walk to the corner store, and stuff our cheeks full of them to see who could hold them in our mouths the longest. I don't even know if he liked the taste or if it was just this thing between us."

These aren't the memories of a three-year-old. I don't remember details from that age, at least. "You come back to see him lots?" I venture. *You can help me do the same with my brother.*

She takes a long, shaky inhale, reaches up and twists the earring in her ear. "Wouldn't you? If you had a ticket back to your safe world, wouldn't you go right now?"

"Yeah." The word chokes me on the way out. God, I miss my family.

"They didn't take that into account, the Embassy," Charlie whispers. "They didn't take a lot of shit into account, but mostly, they didn't consider how most of us were young enough when they sent us away that our safe worlds were the only home we knew, and we didn't even remember Prime. I don't even *know* anyone from my biological family. My great, great, great cousin came to get me because of some death bed promise that had been passed on for generations—out of obligation to her dead father. And all of them expect me to be so damned grateful that they plucked me from *my* home, my chance at being a regular kid in a regular family. They brought me back to a war they've been losing for centuries because they needed more bodies to feed into the machine. Cory doesn't get that. He grew up in Prime. And he's got Lee. I don't have..."

She trails off before she says it. *I don't have anyone.* I want to tell her she has me. I want to be brash enough to say it, but I'm not that guy. *She's only known you for a month, dipshit, and she's way out of your league.* Instead, I say softly "You don't have to explain. I get it, Charlie. Do you ... ever stay long enough for him to *see* you?"

She pinches her lips into a thin line and shakes her head. "Not anymore. When I disappeared, he lost it. He was the only one who remembered me, and he thought he was going crazy when everyone else in the family didn't. The first time I showed up out of nowhere, older than him, it, uh, shook him up pretty bad. He backslid in his therapy. So, now I just leave him these." She points her chin toward the box of cinnamon candy. "It's stupid. I know it is, but I need him to know I'm still here and he's not insane."

"It's not stupid."

"Yeah, it is." She wipes her eyes and straightens like she's bracing for something. Then she sweeps past me and leaves the bedroom.

I tag along. It's the only thing I'm good at.

Charlie stops in front of an open door at the end of the hall, her hands balled into fists.

I look over her shoulder and see the kid from the picture brushing his teeth in the bathroom. He's taller. Shirtless. Looks about twelve years old. His flannel pajama bottoms hang from his hips. Adam's the sort of thin that looks less colt-like and more like something stretched to the point of translucency. One of his hands clutches the porcelain sink and the other rams the toothbrush in his mouth back and forth. He breathes through his nose, inhalations whistling and shallow.

"Adam," Charlie whispers. "It's okay."

He glares at his reflection in the mirror, blue eyes piercing and full of pain behind his white-blond hair. The toothbrush clacks against his teeth. When he peels his lips back, his gums are bleeding.

"Adam, stop." Her voice shakes.

He doesn't. He keeps scouring his teeth like he's scraping off paint instead of plaque. He whimpers as he does it. His eyes flick down to an egg timer perched on the soap holder. When it finally beeps, he spits mostly blood. He rinses it down the drain. It looks strikingly like the foam Riley vomited up before he died. Setting the toothbrush down, Adam grips the porcelain sink, curling over it, shoulder blades sharp and ribs flexing in and out as he gulps air.

Charlie leans close enough to his ear that her cloud of black hair brushes his face. "Hey. I'm here and I love you, okay?"

The kid shudders like someone just tasered him. He reaches a hand up to wipe red flecks of foam from the corner of his mouth. Then he snags the egg timer off the sink, cranks it up to two minutes, and picks up the toothbrush again.

Jesus. I wince as he crams it into his mouth.

Charlie turns around. She speed-walks down the hallway. Before we leave, she deposits a box of Hot Tamales into Adam's backpack, and one more in the tree house in the back yard.

We don't talk at the bus stop. When our ride arrives, it's emptier than the last one and we have the whole back bench to ourselves. Diesel exhaust creeps through an open window, but no-one moves to close it. It's too hot. Charlie sits completely still, her breathing shallow, hands gripping her knees hard. Like something about to flee. Or attack.

Someone smarter than me would know what to say, but I just stare like an idiot at a banner advertisement for MacMillan and Weston Law. Someone's taken a sharpie marker to MacMillan and now he's sporting a handlebar moustache and a monocle.

The engine strains behind us, lurching and wheezing as it grabs gears. It's loud enough that when Charlie speaks, I don't catch what she's saying and have to lean in closer.

"Samantha used to have this tacky sign in our bathroom, 'Every good day starts with brushing your teeth.'" She takes a shuddering breath. "Adam forgot to brush his teeth on the day I disappeared. It's this whole OCD thing now. He can't..." She tucks her head against my shoulder and dissolves into gulping sobs.

I only freeze for a moment before shifting to wrap my arm around her. She lets me and, *Oh God,* it's the strangest feeling. Like I was built just for this. Like the only reason I was ever made was to hold Charlie here, tucked away from a dirty, cruel world she desperately needs respite from. She's alone too. We're the same that way. And I know she's only leaning on me because I'm conveniently here. And I feel like an utter asshole for the excitement tingling down my spine at the warmth of her breath on my neck, but I've never comforted someone like this before, and this is a *real Charlie* moment when she isn't just acting a part, doing her job safeguarding an Embassy asset. I'm not going to let anything mess that up.

She stays leaning against me long after the crying stops. It feels magnetic, like the world would have to fight to break us apart now that we're touching. I don't want it to end. *Maybe she likes you too,* a flicker of hope in my mind prompts. *Maybe you're more than just a job to her.*

It does end, of course. She pulls away from me and wipes her eyes, snagging the *next stop* cable. I try to hold onto the faint smell of leather and bubble gum when the bus sighs to a stop at the next sign, and she gets up and pushes past the smudged accordion doors leading us into the parking lot of a Toyota dealership.

As the bus chugs away, Charlie rips open the other sleeve of her jacket and pulls out a key fob with a Toyota symbol on it. It hums like a mosquito as she clasps it in her hand. I didn't even realize she had another hidden ticket on her. I'm getting used to the constant noise of the ones in the orange pouch.

"Another Corolla?" I ask as we close in on a row with five of the sedans lined up next to each other. These ones are newer and more streamlined than the one in the bunker. A salesman sits in a fold out chair beside the side door of the dealership, cigarette cradled between his fingers. He's smoothing down a crisp shirt that's too tight at his neck and every now and then, he frowns in our direction like he can smell fresh chumps in his lot even though he can't see us. "Doesn't the key have to match the individual car for it to work?" I ask.

"Not as a ticket," Charlie says. "As long as they're close enough, it works. Just like the hotel door key."

We try three cars before we find the one that opens a gateway. And we leave Charlie's safe world.

Chapter Eleven

The new dimension is colder and abandoned. We find a hollowed-out mall. We steal dusty clothes from the rack at a store with broken windows. I grab a thick cable-knit sweater and Charlie takes a hoodie and a couple of blankets. We set up to pass the night in the back office. It's a cinderblock room with no windows and only one exit. We plug all the lights into the power packs and aim them outward before settling in to sleep. I'm starving, but we haven't found any food in this world and Cory was carrying most of our trip rations. We don't have any left.

"David?" Charlie says as I'm dozing off.

"Hmm?"

When she doesn't answer, I roll over. Cold light throws harsh shadows over one side of her face. One pearl stud earring glows like a tiny crescent moon. She's holding something out to me. At first, I mistake it for a ration bar and my mouth waters, but that's not what it is.

It's Everett's tobacco tin.

My neck tingles as I sit up. "You destroyed it. You took it and vaporized it."

"No, I kept it."

Implications fall like acid rain, shocking, stinging me as they strike. "Why? Shit. Charlie, it's still tied to a world full of maneaters. You're supposed to break keystones like that, aren't you? If they find a ticket…"

"They won't," she says. "And if they do, there's still plenty of empty worlds between them and anything they can devour." She nods and looks down at the tin. "You said you used it to go home. I couldn't take that away from you."

Our fingers brush as I reach for it. Suddenly, I want to hold her more than I want a nostalgic souvenir from my world. I've almost scraped together the courage to stroke her fingers when she tightens her grip on the object we're both holding and says, "I need you to do something for me first." Her voice is emotionless. She's switched it effortlessly back into help desk mode.

My heart sinks all the way down to my balls. *God, you're so stupid, David. She doesn't like you. She wants a transaction from you. That's all this is to her. Business.* I let go of the tin and swallow my harsh disappointment. "What do you need?"

"I'll give you this, but you've got to promise to help my brother."

I sigh. "The kid doesn't even know me. And we can't keep going back to your safe world if the Embassy is looking for you there."

"We won't use a ticket. You just proved you can blip without one."

"Charlie, listen to me." I lean toward her, and I do grab her hand now because I'm tired and shutting down and I can't let her lean on me as hard as she's trying to now, because I'll fail. And I don't want to fail her. "I don't even know how I did that."

"Plenty of time to practice. Promise you'll try."

I scrub my eyes and take a deep inhale. "Fine. One condition." *Two can play at this game.* "I'll help your brother if you help me get back home."

"David." She shakes her head. "You know that won't work. There's no way to get you back over there without turning you into a keystone or using a mule. We don't even have a ticket to get you there in the first place."

"I went back without a ticket. You just need to help me figure out how to stay there once I blip over. You know more about this than I do. And I need you to make the Embassy believe I'm dead, so they don't come looking for me."

"How the hell am I supposed to do that?" she asks.

"You'll figure it out, just like I'll figure out how to help your brother."

"Deal." She gives me the tobacco tin.

That night, I visit James again. Whatever this is, it's not like crossing a bridge at all. No temporary invisibility. He can see me right away and he stands beside his Ford Tempo, like always. When we've played our parts, the pavement sucks me under and I can tell that my brother is seeing it, wanting to stop it, but he can't move to help me. Tears roll down his face. I suck in one last breath before the darkness smashes me like a malicious fist. I try to keep my mouth closed, but tar, dirt and rocks cram into my mouth and pack my throat full. Silt fills my ears and creeps under my eyelids. I can't thrash. I can't scream. *Fall through.* My mind screams. *Please fall through. Oh shit. Oh God. Please.* This is how I die, stuck between two dimensions, in a black hole of evil. *I didn't even get to kiss a girl.*

"David!" Cold hands grip my cheeks.

White light burns through my eyelids. The darkness gives me one last disappointed shake before dropping me. I convulse and gulp air.

"Oh my God." Charlie's kneeling over me, forehead pressed to mine, face twisted in anguish. "You stopped breathing."

"I was gone?" I croak.

"Thirty seconds again."

"It was longer on my side. That's not normal, is it?"

"Not normal," she confirms. "When you blipped back you started seizing. Scared the shit out of me. Damn it! You're bleeding. I think you bit your lip." She brushes her thumb over my bottom lip, and it comes away red.

Blood roars between my ears, drowning out any rational thought. I feel drunk. I feel like the darkness is lurking, just out of reach, pissed off that I'm alive. *Show it how alive you are. Fuck the darkness.* "Kiss it better?" The words are out of me before I know what I've said.

She laughs and I smile back to show that I'm joking, but I hold her gaze and reach up and touch her cheek. The invitation is there if she wants it, as ridiculous as it is.

"Let me get a cloth." She pulls away and turns to rummage through her bag.

I deflate. My body still thinks it's been buried alive. My fingers and toes prickle and I can't stop my legs from cramping up. I sit up because the floor feels like a waterbed and I'm still swallowing a messy mix of panic, fear, and letdown. It's easier to breathe sitting up.

Charlie kneels between my legs. She tips my chin up to the light and dabs at my cut mouth.

I can't handle this, her knee brushing the inside of my thigh, the way she bites her bottom lip when she concentrates. My body's still crackling with adrenaline. She's too close and I'm getting a hard on. *Don't let her notice. Please God.*

She doesn't move away when she's done cleaning the wound. Her brown eyes are soft and mischievous as she traces my jaw with cold fingertips. "Better?" She whispers, mouth inches from mine, breath sweet and warm against my face.

"Charlie, don't make me beg."

Her teeth flash as she smiles. Then she leans in and kisses me softly. I stroke the tattoo on her neck, and I kiss her back. *Fuck the darkness.*

Honest to God, I think it *hears* me this time. As soon as the cocky thought burns through me, something clobbers the other side of the storage room door.

We both jump. Before I can process it, Charlie is standing over me with her gun aimed at the entry.

My heart punches into my throat as something rakes down the door outside before wrenching on the knob. An eerie scream echoes in the hallway, the same call I woke up to at the beach on the lake at sunset, the same howl Riley heard just before he died.

Maneaters.

Only this time, there's no dimensional bridge holding them back, just a warped old storage room door.

Charlie shoots a hole in it.

"The fuck are you doing?" I hiss.

"Unplug the lights." She speaks evenly, nodding toward the battery pack beside me with two thick cords plugged into it.

She can't have said what I just thought she did. "What?"

"The lights. Unplug them now."

A black hand whips through the smoking hole in the door, latches onto the wood and yanks back. The image of Riley's chewed-up leg flares in my mind. "No."

She doesn't raise her voice. "You wanna die in here, Sunshine, or do you trust me?"

The maneater shrieks and rams its arm in further, stretching for Charlie, for the orange bag of tickets she wears in her waist bag.

"David, now!" Her order is clipped.

I grab both sockets and yank them out of their plugs. The tiny room plunges into darkness, retinal ghosts of light panels swimming over our heads. The maneater's call cuts off mid-squeal. Then, the door rattles and a flare of red burns my eyes as Charlie's gun discharges.

A heavy body hits the hard floor outside.

"Turn them back on," she says.

I fumble for the battery pack and jab until prongs line up and the LED lights flash back to life. Blood thunders through my head as I plug in the second set of lights.

Charlie looks back to me, eyes narrowing, pressing a finger to her lips.

My gaze locks onto the black hole in the wood. It's the size of a grapefruit. There's no movement or sound beyond it. I hold my breath until my chest burns. When I finally relent, it takes everything in me to match Charlie's even exhalations. Jesus Christ, this isn't the crying girl I held on the bus, or the one who just playfully kissed me. She is stone-cold. All business. A gatekeeper eliminating a threat. The only tension I see in her are the tendons standing out at her neck and her weight shifted to the balls of her feet. Her weapon isn't even shaking as she holds it aimed at the door. How many times has she been cornered like this?

I remember how she charged into the cottage on her motorcycle, right up the porch steps and through the door, flushing out the maneater who'd been dragging me from under the overturned hide-a-bed. She'd been utterly unruffled as she saved my life. I've only seen her crack twice since then, when Riley lost his leg, and today with her little brother.

I wish I could lock down like she does, but I'm pathetic. I have to sit on my hands, so she doesn't see them trembling. How on earth had I ever thought I was military material? I'm not strong enough for this shit. Not strong enough for her. How laughable that moments ago, I'd been cocky enough to think she'd want me. How stupid of me to have this on my mind even now with man-eating aliens prowling on the other side of the door.

When Charlie finally lowers her weapon and creeps back to sit beside me, she must notice my shaky breathing, because she bumps her shoulder against mine and whispers. "I think there was just one."

I lick my lips and nod. "What did you do?"

"Shot it through the eye socket."

"Through the hole you made?"

She smiles. "Yup."

"In the pitch black?"

She wipes her nose and then nods. "They only look through holes if you turn out the lights first. Otherwise, it would have torn down the door and tried to bust our light packs. They're not very smart when they're alone. I don't think they're really whole when they're not in a group."

"Thought this world was empty."

She shrugs. "Yeah, well, you've seen how it is. Some of them like to surprise us and black-market tickets aren't the most reliable. It's not uncommon. Even in abandoned worlds, there's always a few sentries left long after the masses are gone. I don't know what they're watching for, or where they all go after they've devoured a world. Millions of aliens, just gone. Some gatekeepers figure they go back up-tree the way they came. Cory thinks they get hungry enough that they eat each other." She says all this like she's talking about the weather.

"How do you know it's dead?"

"I don't." She cranes her neck toward the door. "It's not moving and it's not calling anymore. I'll make sure it's disabled in the morning."

"What do we do until then?" The question comes out high and more than a little desperate. I know that maneaters call to each other over vast distances using the branch-like frills on their backs like antennas and receivers. Cory said as much. If there's a horde anywhere nearby, they're heading this way now. How can she be so damned cool about this?

How can you be such a fucking coward?

"Tell me about your brother." She interrupts my intrusive thought.

I frown at her, thrown off guard by the change in subject. She's resting the gun between her knees, dark eyes taking me in, oval face serene, giving nothing away. "Why?" I croak.

"Whenever I'm freaked out, I like to think about what I'm doing all this for. It helps ground me."

I scrub the heels of my hands against my closed eyes. "That obvious, huh?"

She bumps my shoulder again. "Don't sweat it. It's your first time up-tree and this hasn't exactly been a routine trip. You're not doing bad for an accelerated initiation, Sunshine. I hid behind a light pack and hyperventilated my whole first mission. How old is James?"

I can't think straight. This is all too much. I'm shutting down. "I don't know. Time's all messed up now, isn't it?"

"How old was he when you left?"

"Twenty-one." *If he's alive. If the maneater venom didn't kill him already.*

"When's his birthday?"

"April 4, 1972. When's Adam's?"

"I don't know. I mean—he didn't know either. His adoption papers weren't complete. He just picked out a day and told me his birthday was the same day as mine. I remember blowing out cake candles together. I don't remember the date though. Just that he lit the candles a dozen times so I could keep blowing them out. There was wax all over the icing by the time we ate it, and Adam didn't care. He ate three slices. He loves sweets."

"James not so much."

"What's his favourite?"

"Food? Toasted bacon, lettuce and tomato sandwiches."

We go on like that forever. It's how we pass the night, passing bits of information back and forth, weaving a safe spot into the dark night with mundane memories of the people we love most. The people we want to save. I know what she's doing. This isn't just about calming me down. Charlie's trying to tie my brother to hers, to convince me that we have a common cause. She doesn't need to persuade me. I want to help her. I can't stop thinking about that kiss.

Chapter Twelve

The next morning, Charlie carves a broomstick into a spear before venturing outside. I hold her gun, backing her up as she cautiously approaches the maneater slumped on the floor. A pair of men's slacks is snagged in the fronds of its back frill, clothes hanger still attached. The body twitches when Charlie stabs it through the eye socket. Frosty air dribbles between its jaws, and a few of its needle-like teeth fall out as she jiggles the spear in its skull to destroy its brain stalk, but there's no intentional movement. Only muscle memory. Her keystone detector doesn't pick up anything when she scans it over the alien's body, so there's no need to dissect it for artifacts, thank Christ. I don't have the stomach for it right now.

We leave quickly, combing the mall for food as we go, with no luck. Charlie doesn't want to spend another night in a building big enough to potentially hide more maneaters, so we scope out a new safe room. She settles on an armored bank truck with operable doors. It's empty inside with room for all our light stands and the sleeping bags we liberated from the mall. I try to blip while I'm awake as Charlie sets up her solar panels for the day.

Holding onto Everett's tobacco tin, I concentrate on every detail of my brother's shitty car, how badly I had wanted him to unpack it and not leave, how thoughtfully he'd filled the survival kit he'd made me. What I'd say to him if he was standing in front of me right now. It doesn't work. Apparently, I'm only capable when I'm unconscious.

After a few hours of trying, we cave and go back to Charlie's safe world. It's a shit idea returning to where the Embassy expects us to be, but there's no food in this world, so if we want to eat, we've got to risk going back to her foster dimension.

At the grocery store, we help ourselves to a rotisserie chicken, a bag of tortilla chips, a seven-layer dip, and a strawberry cheesecake. Plus two cold Cokes to wash it all down. We sit at the smoking area outside and stuff our faces while the world walks by, unaware.

"Can't carry any food back over, so better knock yourself out here." Charlie waves a drumstick at me, a smear of barbeque sauce on her cheek.

"What's the difference?" I speak around a mouthful of hot, tender chicken. "Carrying it over in our bellies versus just carrying it?"

"Dunno." She swigs her Coke. "But, I've tried both. Food doesn't act as a keystone when it's inside us. Breaks down too fast maybe?"

I dip a chip and savour the salty crunch mixed with refried beans, salsa, and creamy avocado. "So, our mission is eat like it's payday, and then leave to sleep it off?" I've got to be honest, I'm not thinking about sleeping. Not after that kiss last night.

"Something like that." She sobers. "I want to show you something before we go."

We get on the bus. We go back to the white bungalow with the lilac tree, but this time it's noticeably bigger and the blooms are fresh, not wilting. There aren't black shutters framing the windows. Instead, there are trellises with climbing roses. I slow to a stop. *We're not in the same world as yesterday.* "Your safe world has different branches?"

"Didn't used to." Charlie stares at the front door.

We go inside. It's midday, but it must be a weekend because everyone's home. The whole family is crowded around the dining room table playing Scrabble. There are three younger kids. None of them look alike, so I'm guessing some of them are adopted or fosters like Charlie was. Adam's there too. At first, I don't recognize him. He's our age, tanned and lean with an easy smile and an open face. He reminds me of a younger version of James, the kind of guy who effortlessly hooks attention and earnestly participates in every conversation.

Charlie's face softens when she sees him. "I like remembering him like this best. In this world, I never came back to visit him. He forgot me like he was supposed to. Has a girlfriend. Making college plans. Look at him."

"He's older."

"The branches aren't quite synced up. Some move a bit faster than others."

"How many others?"

She stares at Adam and her fragile smile drops. "Just one more. Three all together."

"You said there was only one when Prime came to take you home. How do you know that?"

She holds up the battered coin. "This is the ticket they came to fetch me with. I bought it from my cousin a million times removed. Paid through the nose to keep it out of Embassy clutches, and when I came back the first time, there was no loop. It was just one branch—my world—every time I visited."

Charlie's foster mom interrupts with an angry snort that makes me jump. "Chutzpah is not a real word, Adam!"

"Is too," he says. "Look it up."

The dad—Gene I think his name is—picks up a Scrabble dictionary and I gulp hard at the memory of the dictionary Everett had used to send notes into the ether. I wish I'd had a chance to meet the guy and let him know how much he helped me. That he hadn't gone to hell. He hadn't done anything wrong. I wish I was sitting around a table with my family right now.

"Chutzpah. Unbelievable gall or self-confidence," Gene says.

"That sounds about right."

"Thirty-seven points," Adam says smugly.

"What do you think triggered the split?" I whisper to Charlie.

"Me."

I turn to look at her. Her eyes are wide and full of pain. "Don't say that. It wasn't—"

"Yes, it was." Her voice is defeated. Afraid. "I came back. A lot. That one time, when I stayed long enough for Adam to see me, when he freaked out, the ticket started running on a loop after that. It alternated between two worlds. In one, my brother keeps trying to restart the day that he lost me. He can't get over it." She swallows hard and scrubs the back of her neck. "And one is here. He forgot me when I left. He's living a good life. I haven't stolen it from him yet. Haven't messed him up."

"Charlie," I say her name quietly. "You didn't mess—"

"I'll show you the third branch tomorrow. You'll see. I'll mess you up too if you stick around long enough. It's kind of my thing. Brothers. Partners. Everyone really," she says matter-of-factly. We leave after that.

We go back to the armored bank truck and turn on the light packs again. *Every light lit.* We roll out the sleeping bags.

It's cold, but Charlie starts undressing in front of me.

Heat prickles my cheeks, and my gaze drops to my raggedy-ass Converse shoes. "Uh ... you need some privacy?"

"No," she says. "I don't."

Her t-shirt drops to the floor between us and then her bra. It's blue with a tiny embroidered white rose between the cups.

Oh, Christ. This is happening. And I know it's not me that she wants. It's closeness, to *anyone.* I get it. The world's all wrong and she's craving some quick comfort. I'll do in a pinch because I'm here, conveniently smitten with her, and she's concluded that I'm pretty harmless. Also, she's trying to persuade me to help save her brother—and boobs will convince a guy to do just about anything. If I were a real gentleman, I'd already be tactfully deflecting her because this feels driven by all the wrong reasons.

But I'm not a gentleman.

I'm horny. I'm alone in the back of a truck with an attractive and willing girl, and I feel like this offer is on the table for a very limited time. I want so badly to be close to Charlie, and I'll take that closeness any way I can get it. So, I keep my mouth shut and I watch her undress until she's down to just her panties. She's ... something else. Breathtaking is the only word my short-circuiting mind can come up with, all achingly soft curves and deep brown skin. She's way out of my league. I'm getting hard. I can't help it.

"Well?" She crosses her arms over her bare breasts. "I'm not freezing my ass off alone. Show me what you've got, Sunshine."

Charlie's seen me puking. She's seen my bare white ass hanging out of the back of a hospital gown. She's probably seen more than that when I was sedated with IDOCS in every hole I had. *How about you don't think about that right now,* I tell myself as I wriggle out of the borrowed sweater and peel off my t-shirt. I've softened up a bit, but before I decided against a military career, I'd been working my bag off to meet RMC physical performance standards. I'm in decent shape, at least. I unzip and step out of my jeans.

It's cold. We've both got goosebumps on our arms.

I move first, closing the short distance between us to put my hand on her cheek. I'd like to say it's confidence, but that's bullshit. I'm a virgin. Charlie knows it. What else am I supposed to do? It feels idiotic standing before her in my boxers while sporting a painfully obvious erection. So, I kiss her gently, like we did yesterday, trying for a slow start, desperate to not fuck it all up.

She kisses me back hard enough that our teeth click together. Then she grabs a fistful of hair at the nape of my neck before reaching between my legs and gripping my penis. I stifle a gasp.

Okay, no slow start then. Looks like this is going to be a different sort of ride. *Don't finish early* my mind blares. I wish I could remember more but the rest is a blur of breathy moans, blunt fingernails, and the overwhelming urge to fill Charlie up enough that she never feels empty and alone again. It's fast. I back her up against a wall. She wraps a leg around me. We probably break some sort of world speed record.

God, I'm stupid.

I don't know if she comes, or not. She dresses as soon as we finish, leaving me to wonder if this is how it's supposed to feel afterward, like falling through ice, like sand slipping between my fingers.

Like loss.

James is standing by his car, but he looks like shit. His ankle wound has healed up, but he's clutching his duffle bag like he'll blow away without it. Just like the other times, I'm not invisible and he's squinting at me like he knows this isn't a dream.

I smile at him. I can't help it. Even though he looks like he could use about twenty more hours of sleep, he's my brother, and he's stand-ing right here in front of me. I'm holding the canvas survival kit in one hand. The other is crammed into my pocket with a death grip on Everett's tobacco tin. I'm just about to blurt out *I love you* when he says:

"Look, I don't mean to be an asshole, but if you're a ghost or something, I don't have time for this shit right now. Life is fucking nuts, you know what I mean?"

The smile sags from my face. *Yeah, he knows it's not a dream, alright.* I nod. The survival kit feels like a rock in my hand, so I hold it out to him.

"Nah, you keep it," he says. "I made it for you. Just hang in there until I'm done with all these bloody tests, and we'll figure something out, okay?"

I'm good. I want to tell him. *I met a girl. We're on the run together and she's hot and she can shoot a gun and Goddamn she's so kick ass. You'd love her. I miss you so much. Do Mom and Dad even know I'm gone? Tell them they're safe now. Nothing is coming under the door ever again. I fixed it. I promise. And I'm coming home. I'm coming back.* I don't say any of that. Instead, I offer my hand, and when James grips it, I hold my emotion in check and say, "Take care of yourself, Brother."

The road starts to suck me in while he's still shaking my hand. James tries to hold onto me but loses his grip because nothing is stronger or hungrier than the darkness. I try not to fight it. I regulate my breathing, like a free diver about to descend, but my body remembers what being buried alive feels like, and it's having none of it. I freak out before I go under. I lose my shit just as badly as the first time. There's no getting used to this feeling. A black avalanche. A crushing malevolence. A cosmic sentience. I think I know how astronauts feel when they look into the black the first time. The horrible emptiness of outer space. They see it. They know it wants to kill them.

Charlie is cradling my head in her lap when I wake up. The sleeping bags are a twisted mess around us and I'm sweating and hyperventilating. It takes a long time to slow my breathing down. She strokes my forehead, reassuring me that I'm fine and that she's here with me.

"What's it feel like?" she asks when my body finally stops twitching.

I swallow several times before whispering. "It's a cakewalk."

She snort laughs.

God, I love making her laugh. That's the moment I realize it. I'm done for. I'll do anything for her. Anything at all.

It's day three in Charlie's safe world. We don't go to the white bunga-low. Instead, we ride a bus for hours until we hit an industrial looking downtown core. We navigate several streets that I'm thankful to be invisible in, places where you're innately aware of every person walking behind you, where people probably get roughed up and robbed in broad daylight on the regular while their fellow pedestrians quick-walk by.

We enter an apartment complex lobby with cracked glass doors and a wall of mailboxes, half of which have had their doors ripped off. It smells like wet carpet and cigarettes. The intercom doesn't work, and no-one would hear our voices if it did, so Charlie waits for someone to exit the building so we can slip past the locked main door.

The staircase is welded steel with open risers and our steps echo all the way up. Just before we reach the fourth-floor landing, Charlie kneels and reaches under the treads. She pulls out a magnetic key box. We stop in front of 405. The first two numbers are tarnished, their edges caked in paint from the last sloppy renovation. The five is miss-ing and someone has scratched a rough rendition of it into the door.

When we go in, it's dark inside and it smells like a gym locker room. A blond man in a suit is sitting on a couch with a gun in his mouth.

"Shit. Shit. No." The words come out of her high, fast, and running together, like a tea kettle whistling. Charlie lunges into the living room, cracks her shin on the coffee table. She grabs the weapon and tries to wrestle it away from him. "Put it down, Adam. Come on. Adam. No!" She's pulling hard enough that her arms are shaking, but it doesn't make a difference. Her brother doesn't twitch or tense up. He sits there, dead-eyed with tears sliding down his cheeks and the barrel of the gun grazing the roof of his mouth.

"David, help me!" Charlie rasps.

My muscles thaw and I plunge toward them. I wrap my hands over Charlie's and heave downward, but it's like hanging off a brass statue and expecting the metal to give way.

"Come on. *Please!*" she wails. "Adam, don't. Please. Listen to me."

I adjust my grip, hooking my forearm over his and bracing a leg against the couch for leverage. The room fills with the awkward sound of my grunting, and Charlie's strangled begging.

Oh God, he's going to do it. I want to shield her, but when I move, she barks, "Hands on the gun." So, I clamp one hand back over the barrel while the other crushes Charlie's fingers against the handle. Adam's breath puffs hot on my hand. His pale blue eyes widen, and he braces. *No, not in front of her. Please, God.*

Out of nowhere, he lowers the gun. Charlie crumples as he sets it on the coffee table with us still clinging to it. "Don't let go," she gulps.

I keep my hands over hers and we sit there panting, wedged in between the couch and the table, pinning the weapon down between us as Adam lets go of it and leans back. He stares at it for a long time before sucking in a shaky inhale and standing.

Charlie tries to scramble away from his feet, but her brother un-wittingly catches her shoulder with his knee and sends her sprawling.

"Jesus, you okay?" I let go of the weapon and stumble toward where she's curled in on herself on the carpet.

"Don't let go of the gun!" she screeches.

I pivot and clasp my hand back over the weapon on the coffee table just as Adam turns back to it with a small frown. It hits me then, what Charlie is trying to do. My brothers couldn't see the door to Bizarro world as long as I was touching it. It slipped under their radar, and they just lost interest in it. *Adam will forget about the gun as long as we're holding it.*

I scoop it off the table and kneel in front of Charlie as she sits up. She clutches the weapon too, tears squeezing past her tightly-closed eyes. I want to hug her, but I can't let go of the weapon. "I don't know how the safety works on these."

"Just keep it pointed at the floor." Her voice wobbles.

Adam washes his face in the kitchen sink and dries off with a paper towel. He grabs a briefcase, smooths down his tie, and shuffles out the apartment door. Keys jingle and a bolt clunks into place.

Charlie slumps. She holds it together long enough to ease the revolver's hammer down, flip the cylinder out and dump the ammunition. Then she falls into me, wailing.

I clutch her against my chest. "Shhhh. It's okay. It's over."

"He's gotten worse," she blubbers. "He wasn't this bad last time I was here. I mean, I thought, but…"

"It's okay. We stopped him."

"I did this," she howls.

"No."

"I came back again. I'm so stupid. I wanted to talk to him. The happy version of him. I thought if I introduced myself like I was just some random neighbor, he wouldn't make the connection. He wouldn't know it was me. We could talk and he wouldn't freak out."

I'm putting together what she's saying and taking in the apartment at the same time. Tipped over coffee mugs on the floor. Dark stains on the carpet. Empty beer bottles on the kitchenette counter. A small silver frame on the windowsill. A little boy and the washed-out image of the black girl who's hand he's holding. "Adam *knows* you here?" I ask.

"Not as his sister."

"Another split because he met you a second time?"

She nods. "In the second branch. You saw him. He's so happy there. I just wanted to be *near* him, you know?"

"He recognized you?"

"No. He thought I was a new girl at school. We went on a few … dates."

"What?"

She shudders in my grip and speaks her next words into my chest so quietly that I nearly miss them. "He fell for me."

Jesus. "Like, in love?" My words come out flat. I can't stomach the thought of what might be coming next.

"We didn't *do* anything. He's my brother. I was gonna let him down easy, but the Embassy caught up to me first. They interrogated my cousin. She spilled that I'd bought a ticket from her, and they came hunting." Charlie swipes at her cheeks. "This is a closed world. As soon as my detector started picking up a live keystone that wasn't me, I knew they were onto me. I left Adam without saying goodbye and stashed my ticket on my way down-tree. That's when the second split happened, I think."

"They caught you when you went back to Prime?" I ask.

She nods. "I got a letter on my record. Spent some time doing solitary in a hamster ball, but the Embassy needs bodies. Experienced gatekeepers are in short supply." She smiles weakly. "The bastards had to let me back up-tree sometime. Next time I snuck away to check on Adam, there were three worlds. Three versions of him..." she fades out. "I can't lose him, David."

"What are we doing here, Charlie?" I ask carefully.

She sets her brother's gun on the floor and leans back to meet my gaze. "Fixing this. Saving him."

"Charlie..."

She unholsters her own weapon and vaporizes the handgun and its ammunition. The smell of singed carpet permeates the room.

I wrinkle my nose. "It won't stick, will it? The world will reset when we leave, and he'll be back here with that gun in his—"

"I can't do anything else!" Her face twists. "I hide all the sharp knifes. Take his pills. Don't you think I know damned well it's not going to stick for two fucking days? That I'm not scared shitless of coming through that door one of these times and finding him dead. I can't do anything." Her voice cracks. "But *you* can. You can get back here without a ticket now that you've seen it. You can do it without alerting the Embassy. You could take his gun. Talk him down."

"I can't even control when it happens!"

"You promised to help." Her voice drops dangerously. *And I let you fuck me.* She doesn't say that part out loud. Doesn't have to. I can see it in her eyes. "Tell me you'll try," she says.

She's got me by the balls. I like her. She loves her brother and I'd be fighting just as hard for James if I saw him like this. I want to prove to Charlie that I'm capable, that I'm not some stray she has to save over and over again. I want to be the guy that fixes something for her. Something big. I want to sleep with her again—and do it right this time. So, I say yes.

Chapter Thirteen

When we cross into the empty world and make our way to the armored truck, I swear I won't take advantage of Charlie. *She just saw her brother with a gun in his mouth. Stop thinking about how she looks naked.* But we're both too amped up to sleep, and the back of the truck is damned cold.

We're sitting against the wall, huddling under the sleeping bags when Charlie slips her hand into mine. Electricity tingles up my arm, prickling the back of my neck. I do my best to keep my breathing even. Our exhalations fog the crisp air in front of our faces. Her fingers are cold. I can't be this close to her without thinking about how soft her breasts felt last night, how she'd grabbed my hips and pulled me deeper into her any time I tried to slow down. Maybe she thought it was frenetic enough for me not to see the distance in her eyes, that if we fucked hard enough, fast enough, I'd be drowning in a sea of hormones so deep I wouldn't notice the passive set of her face as she looked anywhere except at me. She had started it. It's not like I coerced her. She'd literally grabbed me by the dick and steered me where she wanted. So why did I feel guilty about the way her face closed down when I came inside of her? My Goddamned first time and she'd used me, hadn't she? And she was doing it again now, fingers slipping out of mine to brush the inside of my thigh.

I shiver. I can't help it. "What do you want, Charlie?" I ask carefully.

She doesn't answer. Instead, she moves her hand to my crotch, fingers tracing the shaft of my penis. So, I ask her again.

"Isn't it obvious enough?" she purrs in my ear. "What do you want?"

I want her. I want this to be real, but it doesn't feel like it is. It feels like Charlie playing a part again, like I'm making a mistake. Like I'm *invisible* as she looks past me. I hate it. I can't go back to that. Being invisible. Not with her.

"I want to help you," I say as she strokes me to hardness. "You don't have to ... convince me, okay? I want *you*, Charlie, but only if you want me too. I won't be a job for you. Not like this."

She pushes away hard enough that I wince. Turning from me, she breathes in shallow gulps.

Jesus, I suck at this. I swallow and try to ignore my erection as I shift toward her. "Charlie?"

"What?" she whispers, voice small, like someone who's been lost for long enough, they don't believe it when they hear the searchers calling their name.

"We'll figure this out. I'll get to him, okay? I'll talk him down."

Her body stiffens beside mine. She doesn't answer.

I want to reach out and touch her shoulder but there's this wild and sharp unpredictability about her now, like she might bite my hand if I get too close. So, I just sit there awkward as all hell. My erection wilts. She falls asleep. Or pretends to.

I don't.

I get up and pace, threading between light stands in the cramped rear hold of the truck, holding onto Everett's tobacco tin so tightly that it creaks. My muscles cinch up in the cold. *Come on. You can blip while you're sleeping. How hard can this be? Go to your brother intentionally. Prove to her that you can do it for Adam too.*

I think of James, his eyes always bordered by soft smile lines. How there's this magnetism about him, like he's some minor Greek god capable of captivating men and women with equal ease. That effortless charisma had faded the last time I saw him. He'd looked wrung out and exhausted, but he'd known I was real. He'd spoken to me, taken my hand in his. I still can't shake the look of helpless horror that twisted his face as he tried to stop the pavement from pulling me under.

This isn't working. The more I strong-arm my way toward my brother, the more boxed in I feel. The inside of the truck is too small, the air stale. Charlie's too close, and I'm wound up and agitated. I stop pacing. Static fizzes through my limbs so I take my shoes and socks off. The metal paneling feels like ice, but it grounds me as I stretch my toes and roll my neck until it cracks. I close my eyes and ignore the rectangle afterimage of the closest LED light bank burning behind my eyelids. Slowing my breathing, I pull in each inhalation deep and hold it until my lungs ache, and my ribs stretch.

Instead of concentrating on James, I run my fingers over the rust-pocked surface and embossed letters of the tin. I trace the rolled seam of the lid. I let my mind wander and imagine every exhalation pulling wisps of me out of it, unthreading my organs and evaporating my bones until I'm vaporous enough to absorb into the pores of the metal.

The universe is made up mostly of empty space. I remember that much from school. The Andromeda galaxy is on a crash course with our Milky Way but in four or five billion years, when those spirals plow into each other, it's unlikely that any stars will collide. There's just so much space between them. So. Much. Space. All I've got to do is drip in between, sieve into another world, dance between atoms.

It feels like dozing at first, like my mind clings onto the armored truck on spider web threads. I can hear Charlie's breathing. The LED lights glow red past my closed eyes. The floor feels solid and icy under my feet, but my body pulls me somewhere deeper, quieter, like it knows the way. My breath crystallizes high in my chest, my organs quiver, and then everything goes absolutely still.

My feet are on carpet, threadbare stuff with foam underlay that's been pulverized to sand by countless heels. The air is warmer, humid. It smells like sleep and something saccharine and medicinal. I open my eyes. I'm facing a desk. A textbook lies centered neatly on the worn tabletop. I touch it and it feels solid, laminated cover peeling, its corners worn off. It's titled *Metallurgy – Residual Stress and Distortion*. This is a bedroom, a dorm room, I realize as I turn. I'm not outside our house on the day James packs his Ford Tempo for school. Not stuck in a memory. This is new. *Holy shit.* I cram both my hands into my pockets, one of them gripping Everett's tin like a lifeline.

The ceiling panel above the bed has been knocked ajar. A black triangular maw yawns into the suspended space above. A broom lies amongst the crumpled sheets along with several plastic cough medication containers full of purple syrup. Empty bottles of the stuff lie discarded haphazardly on the carpet. Too many empty bottles. My chest cinches tight, and fear loosens my guts.

No. No, no, no. Not this. Not him. James isn't like this. But there he is, leaning against the door, head drooping, a wraithlike sleepwalker, too pale and too thin. He's breathing like a wind-up toy on its last few slow ticks before it seizes. A splatter of purple syrup streaks down his shirt.

Oh God, please. I can't move. My body is still settling into itself, knees locked, nerves fried.

James's head bobs up and his gaze latches onto me.

I break inside. There's almost nothing left of the strong, carefree older brother I knew. He's chewed up and sucked dry. His eyes are glassy, pupils too small, but I can tell he sees me by the small moan he makes, the way his neck tenses up.

Talk to him. Say something. It takes everything I've got to keep my voice steady.

"What are you doing, James?"

"Surviving." His lip curls as he slurs the word.

Something in me snaps. My mind plugs into my body and I'm fully here. I can move. I use the anger and fear swelling in my core to fuel a lunge across the room toward him. "Bullshit," I spit. "You're better than this. Hell, I wished I was you. Don't you dare do this to me, you hear? Don't you fuck up how I remember you." His gaze moves over me, eyes slow in their restlessness, like he's lounging in an ice bath and long past the point of shivering.

He's overdosing.

Panic snaps through me as I lean closer. "Do you hear me?"

He blinks. It's several seconds before he shakes his head.

"This isn't surviving. This is you killing yourself and hiding it behind that fucking golden boy smile. You some sort of masochist?" My words are full of fire. It squelches the cold terror needling my insides. *Come on, James. Rise to the bait. Talk to me. Just keep talking.*

"No," he slurs, raising his chin defiantly. "Am I s'posed to keep calm and carry on? You know it's wrong over here. You're gone and there's just this ... this hole. The world keeps trying to cover it, but we can feel it—Mom, Dad, all of us. No matter how much it tries to make us forget."

My shoulders drop. Heat rushes through me, pulsing behind my eyes, making my vision swim with hot tears. *He hasn't forgotten me. They remember.* My family. They know I'm gone, and they miss me. *I'll mess this up.* I know it deep in my bones. If I stay here too long, James's world will shred into different variations and none of them will be right or whole. None of them will be him. Not fully.

Fix this. He's strong enough to survive maneater venom, and he's not freaked out that you're here. Don't let him think of you as a missing puzzle piece. Convince him he's whole without you or he's not going to survive until you get back. Tentative relief threads through me as I lean into a plan. My voice is thick with emotion but firm with conviction. "It's okay to forget. You can let me go, man. You've got to."

The room sucks inward. The floor sags like a trampoline. Carpet fibres scratch my feet and pool around my ankles as black gravity coalesces beneath me. *Oh, Christ not yet. I need more time.* I plead with the darkness.

"No," My brother barks, teetering away from the door. "I'm s'pose to save you."

I slam a hand against his chest as he falls forward. My feet sink deeper, but I grit my teeth, clutch his shirt front with one hand, and reach around him to haul the door open. If I can get him into the hallway, if we can make enough noise, someone will hear it. Someone will come help before the blackness swallows me.

"I'm s'pose to..." James's voice is deep, broken.

Cough syrup bottles clatter around us as I wade through them, swimming in the floor like it's a peat moss swamp while my brother's feet skate across the top. I paste on my best reassuring smile and speak in his ear as I press him back. "You don't have to save me this time, James. It's my turn. I promised. I'll keep the darkness from swallowing you up."

His eyes flare open. "Wait," he says, digging in his heels, but I'm running out of time.

Bracing as the world liquifies around me, I tackle James hard. Air barks out of him as he flies into the hallway, smashing into the opposite wall hard enough for the panelling to crunch.

I wince as he goes limp and puddles to the floor.

"James?" A muffled voice calls his name, alarmed.

Oh, thank Christ, someone else is here. Relief swamps me and the blackness squeezes its coils tighter. "Live." My voice cracks. "Stop this shit."

Feet thump. A bedroom door down the hall rattles open.

James gapes at me, petrified. "I don't even know your name," he blubbers.

The darkness is fast, hungrier than I've ever felt it. *This is the last time I'll ever see him.* The thought strikes me with calm certainty. *The last time I'll ever see anybody. I pressed too far and it's going to kill me.* "It's okay, James," I blurt before blackness wrenches me under.

And then it's in me, slipping between all of my spaces, filling them with matter so dense my thoughts implode in snapping succession. My lungs collapse. Tendrils of something leaden and cold slither through all my veins and capillaries, stroking my insides like the IDOCS did. Whatever this is, it won't kill me fast. I know that now that it's inside me, sharing its malevolence. It's something that likes to play with its prey, something that delights in dying more than death, a darkness that sucks on suffering like it's drawing marrow out of bones. Seconds ago, I was sure that being buried alive was the worst possible outcome of this, but now it knifes through me, sharp glass ripping through my insides and poisoning everything with crippling fear in its wake.

There's something far worse than dying buried in the black.

Not dying.

The blackness is holding me here suspended, crossing all my wires so that I live when I shouldn't, crushing me and letting me feel every sensation of my consciousness smearing and my bones warping while it leaches into me, fossilizing me in place. Whatever it is that modulates pain in my brain is pulverized. I feel it all. Agony isn't the word for it. Torture doesn't come close.

Hell.

This is hell.

That's what the blackness is.

Everett was right. We opened a door to hell. And now I can't get out. I can't... Please, I ... I want ... to ... die.

Chapter Fourteen

My head feels like it's in a vice. My body hurts all over and there's this awful astringent taste in my mouth. Iron and something else. I spit blood and try to sit up, but I'm too dizzy and my face feels numb. The smell of urine fills my nose, and it dawns on me that I've pissed myself. My ears are ringing so loudly, I can't hear what the person leaning over me is saying. I wave them away, angry that they've woken me.

But they ignore me, fingers bright with blood, pressing a cloth against the side of my mouth, calling my name over and over. Why won't they stop? I frown and try to roll away from them. I'm tired. I don't want to wake up yet and they can't take a damned hint.

The whole left side of my face thumps in time with my heart. "He needs ... help," I croak.

"I'm here. I'm helping, Sunshine. Stay with me."

Sunshine? I frown. "James needs ... me."

"Yeah, well he can't have you if this is how he gives you back," she murmurs under her breath, wiping her bloody hands on her pants. Pearl earrings. Charlie.

"Where are we?" I wince at the racks of light leaning over us like curious bystanders. Something lumpy cushions my head. The sleeping bag. It's bloodied too.

"In an empty world. Back of a truck. You're safe, okay? Just don't move." Charlie twists a pouch in her hand until it crackles. She presses it against my face, and I baulk at how cold it is. *Ice pack. It's an ice pack, stupid.* Shame creeps over me like spiders I can't brush off. *You pissed your pants.*

"Where are we?" I blurt. They're the only words my mouth seems to know right now.

"You fell. Hit your head, but you're back now." She brushes hair away from my eyes.

"James." My face crumples. *God, you're an idiot. Stop this. Don't cry.*

"You can't help him right now. Come back to me first, okay?"

"Where are we?" I want to ask anything else, but my tongue can't make the right shapes. It's swollen and clumsy.

"We're in a safe place. Let's just stay lying down for awhile, okay?"

Black leaches out of my pores, dribbling back into the floor. I can't see it, but I feel it. God, I'm so tired, but something's niggling in my brain, a worm of a thought that won't let me go back to sleep. "The tin?" I ask.

"What?" Charlie leans close enough that her hair brushes my flushed cheek. It smells like oranges.

It's too hot in here. I swallow the chemical taste in my mouth. "The ... tin. Where?" I reach for my jean pockets, but my fingers are clumsy, and I can't feel the reassuring hardness of the tobacco tin when I pat down fabric. *Oh god, I'll never get back to him.* Tears pool in my eyes, streaking down my sweating face. "I lost it. Aw, shit."

"It's okay, David. Calm down, alright?"

But I can't. It's gone. I lost Everett's tobacco tin, dropped it when I tackled James, or lost it to the blackness in the in-between. I can't save my brother. I just learned how to reach him, really reach him, and now... I can't go home. "I fucking lost it," I blubber like a two-year-old, because that's what I am when I'm with Charlie. A toddler. A lost dog. Utterly useless.

I hyperventilate.

She pulls the other sleeping bag over and lies beside me, brown eyes snapping with authority, one hand pressing the ice pack to my face and the other swiping tears from my cheek. "Breathe with me, David," she says, inhaling through her nostrils. "Big breaths. Come on." She pulls my shaking hand to her chest and presses it flat against her sternum. "Come on. Big breath in."

I take a shuddering gulp of air.

"Again," she says, exhalation warm against my cheek. "Slower this time."

I anchor myself to her voice, the openness in her face.

We lie curled into each other amidst the mess on the floor of the armored truck. It takes a long time for me to get my breathing under control and when I do, exhaustion creeps over me, heavy and heady. Charlie tells me I need to stay awake for a bit. Something about a concussion. She asks if I need help changing and I tell her no, but it takes every last stitch of energy I have to kick off my soiled clothes and wrestle into clean ones.

She keeps her back turned as I do. Then she wipes up the blood on the floor with my dirty shirt before sitting down beside me again.

I feel dizzy. Drunk and horribly hungover at the same time. My fingers probe at the swollen lump on my cheek. My cut tongue throbs in my mouth. "Seizure?" The word drips out like syrup.

Charlie nods. "You fell. Hit your head. It made an awful sound. Woke me up."

"I did it."

"Did what?"

"I went to him, while I was awake." I need for her to know I'm capable of more than pissing my pants and biting my tongue.

Fragile hope widens her eyes. "You blipped?"

"Somewhere different this time. James's dorm room. He was in trouble, and it was real. He could see me. I could touch him. I could ...

move him." I don't tell her about how he looked like a corpse already, how my bright and brilliant brother was overdosing in front of me, and I don't know whether or not my actions saved him. She saw her brother with a gun in his mouth today, and then she saw me seizing on the floor, blood foaming from my mouth. I've burdened her enough for one day. So, I muster up the last of my strength and say, "I can do it, Charlie. I can take Adam's gun. I can talk to him, and he'll hear me. I just need a keystone."

She pulls at one of her earrings. Tears fill her big brown eyes, but this time, she doesn't turn from me. She doesn't shut down. A desperate, relieved laugh bursts out of her and she strokes my cheek. "My God, you're something, Sunshine. Really something." It's her. Charlie with her shields down, hardness melted, mouth soft. She leans forward and kisses me on the forehead, and it's a real moment. Not choreographed. Not rehearsed. Just. Her.

I should stop talking. A smart person would stop talking now, but I'm exhausted and whatever filter I may have had has burned out. A sheepish smile perches on my face, and I hear the crass words leak out of me. "How come you only like me when I'm a broken pile of shit?"

She coughs out a laugh. "We're all broken piles of shit. Maybe I like fixer-uppers."

"I like you all the time."

"You shouldn't." She pulls her hand back. Puts it in her pocket. Her eyes go steely. The walls are going up again, and I want to hold onto her, to kiss her, but my body feels clumsy and uncooperative. "I'm not a good person," she says.

"Don't." I cringe at how utterly broken my voice sounds.

"Don't what?" Her brow creases.

"Don't mask. Please, just ... be here. With me." I reach for her hand, and she lets me take it. "I want *you*, Charlie, not whoever you're pretending to be for them."

I don't remember falling asleep, but next thing I know Charlie's nudging me awake, asking me to sit up. I groan as I do. All my muscles hurt worse than they do days after a heavy workout.

"Shit. I was supposed to keep you awake." She groans, eyes bleary. Then she rummages in her bag. I wince as she shines a penlight into my eyes. "Okay. We're okay. Pupils reactive and equal. Tell me where we are."

"Disneyland."

She raises her eyebrows.

"You don't have Disneyland?" I say aghast. "Oh, you've got to come to my world. We're going to Disneyland together. I can't wait to see you with mouse ears on."

She looks at me for a long second before saying "Be serious. I'm trying to make sure your brain isn't swelling."

I squint at the flat metal walls around us. "We're in the back of a bank truck."

"How's your face feel? Your cheek's bruising already."

I stretch my jaw. "It's sore. Nothing major, I don't think. How long did we sleep?"

"A couple hours, I think. It's not dawn yet. Tell me the months of the year in reverse order."

"Nobody knows that before dawn," I yawn.

"Humor me."

I list them off and then ask if I can go back to sleep.

When I wake up, Charlie's sleeping against me, warm body pressed against my back, gentle breath tickling my neck. I roll toward her slowly enough that she doesn't wake. My body feels like it ran a marathon, but my mind is clearer, and the glare of the LED lights don't hurt like they did before.

Charlie's hair sticks to the stubble on my chin and I stroke it away from her face. It feels like the most natural thing in the world, holding her like this. I can't stop staring at her. She's a rumpled, unguarded mess when she sleeps, hair squashed against her cheek, t-shirt twisted around her ribcage, blankets tangled between her legs. I think she's the most beautiful thing I've ever seen. I've never been this close to someone. Not like this.

The air is icy, and she presses closer to me in her sleep. I tuck her head under my chin and wrap my arms around her. I can tell the exact moment she wakes up by how she stiffens in my embrace, but I pretend to sleep because I don't want it slipping through my fingers. This feels like something I won't be able to get back once it's gone, and I've never had it, Goddamnit. Is it too much to ask for? A few hours of uncomplicated intimacy. A sacred bit of normalcy in between the moments that feel like death.

She doesn't move, but her breaths shorten into guarded exhalations against my chest. It's a long time before she whispers. "You don't want to do this."

"Do what?"

"Fall for me."

"Who says I'm falling for you?" I whisper into her hair. "Maybe I'm just using you for your kick ass first aid skills."

She snort laughs and slaps my chest lightly. "I'm serious."

"I am too. I'm falling a lot lately."

"Hmmm. Speaking of, let me see your eyes." My heart sinks as she reverts to business mode.

I shift back and look at her dutifully as she peers into each of my eyes in turn.

She nods, apparently appeased. "How's your tongue? Any bleeding?"

"It's fine." I hate this. She's right here, still in my arms, and I'm going to lose this moment because I don't have the balls to make the first move.

"Let me see." She frowns.

Fuck it. I cup her chin, lean in, and when she doesn't pull away, I kiss her softly.

Her breath catches. Her lips part.

I kiss her again, running my fingers over the lines of the tattoo on her neck, tasting her as she opens her mouth to me. She's tentative, careful, so I am too. I flick my tongue against hers, lightly suck on her bottom lip, and then I pull away smiling softly. "See? Tongue operable."

"Apparently," she says breathlessly. Her finger traces my jaw, but her eyes are already unfocused, distant, worried.

"Charlie," I whisper. "Please look at me."

She does. It takes a moment, but she does.

"I've been invisible for a long time. Sometimes, I ... I suck at reading people. If you don't want..." I swallow and try again. "Tell me to stop, and I'll stop. I don't want to fuck it up this time."

"You didn't fuck it up last time," she murmurs, fingertips feathering over my bruised cheek. She's lying.

"I would have liked to have been more ... considerate."

"You would have been. If I had let you drive." She grazes her fingernails down the back of my neck. "But I set the pace. And you followed."

"So, let me drive." I hold her gaze. "Let me do something for you. I'm a quick learner."

"Don't you dare fall for me," she gulps.

I flash her what I hope is a confident grin. "Don't tell me what to do when I'm driving."

She smiles and she lets me in.

I make love to Charlie on the floor of an armored bank truck and this time I worship her. I undress her like she's a goddess. I taste the salt of her neck, ache at the sight of her soft breasts, brush my lips over her stomach, her hip bone, the inside of her thigh. I ask her how she likes to be touched and she guides my hands. We move in and out of each other like a tide, teasing each other toward the shore. She's so perfect it hurts, short nails, strong legs, dark skin, brown eyes drinking me in and taunting me in turns.

I never understood why sculptors spent hours recreating women in marble, not until now. They're trying to capture this. This magic. Smooth shoulders, delicate back muscles, elegant neck, all of them impossibly soft. I'm light-headed at the sight of her.

My fingers are lost in her warmth. She grips me, but I pull her hand away, pin it over her head. "Wait, please." I rasp, holding back. I'm hard, throbbing, and on the edge of coming, but I don't want to yet. I want her. I need to hear my name on her lips, want her to sound hungry when she says it, want to bring her to the edge with me and hold her there until our blood howls in our ears.

She kisses me deeply enough that the cut on my tongue hurts, but it's a good pain, clean and mind-clearing. She's shivering, arching into my hand as I stroke her. I brace over her as she grabs me, guides me into her and thrusts her hips to take me in. She's all heat and urgency, wrapped around me like a storm, breath thundering in my ears.

"David, please," she moans, and I lose control.

She clutches the hair at the back of my neck.

I cry out and bury myself in her over and over again until there's this massive release between us, and I can feel her muscles gripping me in waves. She fills up the emptiness the darkness left behind. I breathe her in, lay my head on her chest, and listen to her heart thumping strong and fast in my ear. This is what it feels like when people say someone else is their entire world. Like sunshine through a window. Morning when no-one else is awake yet. Planets pulling at each other's orbits.

We go soft against each other. I shift onto my side and pull her against me. The cold creeps over our skin and I draw one of the sleeping bags over us. She lies, tucked in the crook of my arm. She doesn't shut down. Doesn't leave. "Thank you," I murmur.

She lifts her head, wrinkles her nose "*Thank you?*"

I'm swimming on the edge of sleep, utterly relaxed and unguarded. "I'm new at this. Not proper bedroom etiquette to thank someone for mind-blowing sex?"

She smiles. "Mmmm. Maybe a mint on my pillow next time and a personalized card."

"To Charlie: Thank you for going above and beyond in your first aid efforts."

"To David: You are cordially invited to drive again any time you like."

I grin.

She lays her head on my chest, and something pokes me. I flinch hard enough that she jerks back.

"What?" she says.

"Your earring." I reach up and the pearl stud in her right ear falls into my hand as I touch it. "The back's come off."

Her face drops as she stares at it. I can't place the emotions swirling behind her eyes, but it's something dark. "What?" I ask.

"That's it." She stares unblinking at the pearl in my palm. Her throat works. "Your keystone. The one that will get you to Adam. He gave these to me before I left. I kept them." Before I can protest, she adds "They're too small to be live keystones, I've scanned them to be sure. They don't hold open bridges. But you don't need a bridge, do you, David?"

"I don't need a bridge." I roll the earring in my hand and terror cuts at my insides as I think about being swallowed by the dark again. Every time, it feels like it's examining me, studying how I'm put together by taking me apart.

I've got to do the same.

The only way I'll get home—and stay there—is if we find another keystone linked to my world, and then I learn enough about how the darkness works to escape its clutches permanently. Charlie will help me do that if I help Adam. I can convince him that his sister is real, that she loves him, and that none of this is his fault. I can learn how to control my ability enough to get me back where I belong. With James and Dad and the rest of my family.

Home.

Funny thing that. The more time we spend together, the more Charlie feels like home. Is that the world erasing my family, or is it me?

Chapter Fifteen

We prepare as much as we can. We go to the grocery store in her safe world and eat. Charlie keeps her eyes pinned to her scanner the whole time we're there, looking for unfamiliar keystones that would indicate an Embassy retrieval team coming for us, but hiding out up-tree while time charges on at a breakneck pace down in Prime seems to be working out for us. We're the only blips on the screen and so far, the headaches are manageable. Charlie says they'll get worse the longer we stay up-tree.

When we blip back, we go back to the abandoned mall and search until we find a first aid kit, which we rob for supplies. Charlie pulls an automated external defibrillator out of a faded cabinet in the food court and jabs at the power button, but the machine doesn't respond.

I gape at her while she tucks the AED and two sets of pads and cables into her bag. "What?" she says. "You stopped breathing the time before last. We want to be ready, don't we?"

"The batteries are dead. Do you even know how to use it?"

She shrugs. "I have power packs. I can wire it to another source so long as the capacitors are good, and you don't have to know how to use them. They're made for emergencies. They're practically idiot proof."

"That's incredibly reassuring," I say.

We return to the armored truck and clean it up as much as we can. Charlie helps me scour the cargo area for the tobacco tin, but it's nowhere to be found. My chest twists tighter at that. It's lost. I had my way home in my hands and I lost it. It feels insurmountable, like something too heavy for me to handle right now, so I don't handle it. It's easier to go numb instead and save that problem for later.

One bridge at a time, David.

Charlie wires the AED to one of her battery packs and when she presses the power button this time, it lights up and an indifferent woman's voice instructs, "Apply pads to patient's bare chest. Plug in pads connector next to flashing light."

"There." Charlie beams, forced brightness almost covering the nervousness in her voice. "Not IDOCS, but it's here if we need it."

We push the light stands to the back of the truck and cover the wheel wells with the new sleeping bags we liberated from the decrepit department store dominating the west end of the mall. Ones not yet splattered by my own blood.

Then I sit cross-legged on the floor in a space that feels more like a sanitarium than a truck. I hold Charlie's earring in my hand, and I close my eyes. Slow my breathing. Five minutes pass. Ten.

Her feet scuff behind me as she paces. Watching. "Does it hurt?" she asks with a softness that contradicts her impatient stride.

"When I go? I barely feel it. It hurts to come back. It feels like..." I'm about to try for a joke but the words die on my tongue. It's not often that I'm too scared for humour. Charlie's waiting so I fall back on honesty instead. "Like dying, suffocating in an avalanche. Something tries to hold me there."

"Something?"

I don't open my eyes. "Darkness, but worse. It feels sentient. It wants to hurt me."

"Why come back at all then. Why not stay?"

That's the plan, as soon as I learn how. I can't tell her that. I can't think about how it will wreck Charlie when I go, how I'll be abandoning her like everyone else in her life has. Instead, I grip the earring until it jabs into my palm, thinking of James splayed like a car wreck casualty in his dorm hallway, his eyes rolling back, and his body going slack as the floor swallowed me. I don't even know if he lives. I'll never know if I don't figure out how to beat the darkness. My throat tightens and I push the words out. "I can't control it. The world turns to quicksand and sucks me in. It's like I'm under the radar for a bit, and then it finds me, and I'm just ... under."

"Buried alive?" she asks quietly. "That's how you come back?"

Fear is soaking in, and I feel like I'm under water. I open my eyes and look over my shoulder. "Can we not talk about it right now?"

She winces. "Sorry."

"What do you want me to say to him?" I'm the one in business mode now, shedding all the emotion from my voice, ignoring the tingling in my hands and feet.

"Just tell him you know me. Show him the earring if he needs proof. Let him know I'm safe and I love him." Her words pinch off and a strange jealousy ripples through me.

He's her brother. Get your head on straight. "Where does he keep the gun?" I ask.

"Nightstand by his bed."

"Any other weapons I should know about?"

"I move the knives from the block in the kitchen when I go. And there's painkillers in the bathroom medicine cabinet."

For a moment, I don't follow her. Then I realize that while I'm worried about getting shot or stabbed as I materialize in her brother's apartment, Charlie's concerned about potential instruments of suicide.

A cruel thought lances my mind. *Your safety isn't her priority. She MacGyvered a goddamned defibrillator.*

I ball up the mess of thoughts swarming in my head and try to reset.

I promised to do this. She wants to save her brother same as I want to save mine and Adam is the only one I can reach right now. I can do this. For her. And then she'll help me.

It takes a long time to slow my heart rate. My mind flicks over what details of Adam's apartment I can recall. Threadbare couch. Cramped kitchenette. Empty beer bottles clustered on the counter. The water-stained childhood picture of Charlie and him on the windowsill. Then, I let it all go and turn my attention to the pearl earring.

I imagine it getting bigger, like a craterless moon. I picture the tight layers of nacre cocooning an irritant. I think of myself in layers too, unravelling until my muscles are too light to hurt, my bones are smoke, and my brain is more energy than mass.

My insides feel like cotton candy dissolving in water. Something hooks into my ribcage and tugs. The world goes static.

I'm sitting on carpet.

Stale air fills my nose, the smell of greasy take out, and dirty laundry.

I'm in Adam's apartment.

My body feels like someone snipped all my nerve endings and then heavy-handedly twisted them together again. I'm sluggish, scattered. And then everything syncs up. My eyes fly open. I scramble to my feet, scanning the living room with blood whooshing between my ears, expecting a gun to my head, a knife in my belly—or worse yet Adam dead and decomposing on his couch.

But the room is empty.

I'm standing where Charlie and I held the gun together. Cocking my head, I strain to hear any sign of human life elsewhere in the apartment. I wait for five long breaths, but everything's still. I'm alone. Dust motes swirl through a bar of sunlight slashing the living room. I pocket Charlie's earring, shoving it down deep to make sure I don't lose it, and then I head down the short hallway.

The bedroom door is open. There's no noise from the attached bathroom, so I creep in and stare at a fastidiously made king size bed. Matched navy pillowcases. Severely tucked comforter. It seems out of place compared to the shabby living room that's littered with evidence that Adam lives. This doesn't look lived in at all. It doesn't even look like he sleeps here. I go to the nightstand and the gun is in the drawer, just where Charlie said it would be. There's relief in that. It wouldn't be here if he offed himself already, neither would the clutter in the living room. The place would have been gutted and sanitized if Adam were dead.

I pick up the revolver.

Now what? I don't have Charlie's weapon to destroy it, and a horrible dread is crushing the air out of me. I can't get enough air. The gun shakes in my hands. My vision swims as I glance at my feet, but the floor is solid beneath me. *Oh shit. Not a panic attack. Come on.*

I didn't expect this. I'm scared of the darkness, but I didn't expect the anticipation to cripple me before it even arrived. My body remembers death, and it doesn't want to visit it again, has absolutely no interest at all in learning more about it. Coiling up and pumping adrenaline through me, it rips the reins from the logical part of my brain and freezes me in place. *Come on, breathe. Just breathe. Move.*

But my legs are locked. It feels like someone's standing on my chest. Anxiety hooks through my ribs, clamps over my heart and squeezes.

I fight it. Lean into the bed and suck in air. *Just get out of the apartment. Hide the gun somewhere.*

I stumble out of the bedroom, ricocheting off the walls. Panting.

When I reach the kitchenette, the whole world rolls sickly and the linoleum sucks on my feet. "Shit!" I hiss. Forgetting the knives, I slog toward the door, crank the deadbolt and crash into the complex hallway. Adam's apartment is near the end. It's a bare corridor except for the red metal fire hose cabinet in the stairwell. I lunge for it.

It feels like walking on a waterbed. Stabilizing against the wall, I wade through an unravelling world that's up to my shins now. My feet feel numb. The blackness slackens and then jerks me further in, like a predator adjusting its grip. I stumble right before I reach the cabinet, right hand clutching the top edge, nails scraping and then catching a seam. The one on my index finger rips clean off. The sound of my own fingernail clattering onto the metal top drives nausea through me. The pain is instant and incredible. I grab onto the cabinet handle and yank it open, as my nerve endings scream, and blood runs down my hand.

Shoving Adam's revolver in between the stiff folds of the fire hose, I slam the cabinet closed, bear-hugging it, drawing up my legs as the blackness opens up beneath me. But there's no escaping it. This isn't a childhood game. The floor isn't lava, and the blackness isn't stupid.

The whole floor bubbles toward me. The hallway is an amoeba, and I'm its twitching prey. Darkness claps into me from all sides and I scream. It fills my throat and sets like cement in my lungs, and you'd think I could bolster myself against it. You'd think knowing what to expect would prepare me somehow, and I could draw on some sense of calm inevitability, the sort of peace people settle into just before they die. But there's none of that. I'm incapable of meeting the darkness with logic. My body panics as thoroughly as it did the first time. It rails against death as strongly as it always has. And the blackness holds me there, whispering murky promises.

One of these times, it won't let me go. One of these times, I won't slip through its grasp. It'll pin me like a bug and examine me for all eternity, pulling my limbs off one by one. But this time, I fall through right as I'm losing consciousness.

I wake like a baby being born, red, bloody, and screaming. Something is holding me. I swat it away, elbow out of its grasp, and scuttle back until I smack into a wall. The floor is wrong. Soft and tangled. I don't know where I am, who I'm with, only that I'm in danger and something's trying to kill me.

"David," a low voice speaks.

My gaze snaps to her. She's haloed by harsh light that burns my eyes. Cloud of black hair. Leather jacket. Strong open face. I know her. "Charlie?" I whimper.

"You're safe. You're back."

Home? No. Keystone, my mind blares. *Make sure you didn't lose it.* I reach for my pocket only to brush the exposed nail bed against fabric and send pain hissing up my arm. I yelp and gaze down at my bloody hand.

"What happened?" She eases toward me through a mess of sleeping bags.

"Don't," I blurt, covering my ears with my palms and squeezing my eyes closed. It's too bright. Too loud. Her voice echoes like feedback in my skull. I want to puke.

"What can I do?" she asks.

"Don't ... talk." I choke. My chest feels like my ribs are ratcheting tighter, and I can't process anything else past the ringing in my head. *Breathe. Just get some air in. Jesus Christ, that was awful. You're not getting better at this. You're getting worse.*

I try to breathe, but it feels like sucking through a straw. My hands tremble no matter how hard I press them against my ears. I recoil when I feel Charlie settling beside me, but she doesn't speak, just breathes with me, her long exhalations guiding me back to the shore of this world like a rower's smooth, practiced strokes.

It's a long time before I feel I can let my hands drop without my skull breaking. Sweat plasters my hair to my forehead. It itches as it trickles down my sides. I feel like a horse that's been run until it collapsed. My finger throbs angrily.

"Can I see it?" Charlie asks in a whisper.

I hold out my hand. The exposed nailbed looks like a chunk of raw steak.

Her fingers are cool and gentle as she wraps a loose bandage around it. "What happened?" she asks again.

I freaked out. "I fell," I croak. "He wasn't there. I hid his gun in the hallway."

"The hallway?" She tries to muffle the disappointment in her voice and fails. "What about the knives? The pills?"

I shake my head.

She sighs and sits back, rubbing her temples.

Heat ignites deep in my belly. I turn to level a hard gaze at her. *Jesus. She has no idea.* "I'm sorry. I couldn't squeeze much in between almost dying and almost dying."

"No, I'm sorry. I didn't mean—"

"It's nothing like travelling through a gate, Charlie. I know you think I'm soft but—"

"Soft! Jesus Christ, David. I never said that. You survived seventeen years in a hostile world. Nobody's done that. Ever. Eighteen days trapped in a hamster ball with *me,* with nothing but IDOCS holding you together. And you didn't lose your shit when Riley... You haven't complained once on this crazy fucking trip. You just roll with the punches. You're not soft. I'm sorry. I just..." She takes a deep breath and turns from me. "I hate not being able to do anything but wait. I wish I could go instead of you."

Dread opens up in me at the thought of the darkness reaching out for her. "Charlie." My voice is so hoarse, so pathetically desperate that her gaze meets mine again. "I'd go a hundred times to stop you from going once."

She doesn't say anything after that. She hands me a couple of painkillers and I dry swallow them and then doze against the wall. I think she puts one of the sleeping bags over me, because later, I wake up under one with no recollection of pulling it over myself. My whole hand throbs, but my body's settled into heavy exhaustion when I announce, "I'm going back."

She straightens from reorganizing the first-aid kid. "Now? Shouldn't you wait?"

"I was too keyed up before. I'm tired now. Calmer. I don't want to wait until I'm rested enough to know better." I smile softly even though the thought of going back makes my back go rigid. I can't leave it alone. I *need* to learn how to do this better if I want to go home.

"I've patched you up enough for one day." She tries, but I know she really wants me to go. There's no socially appropriate way to tell someone that you'd like them to take another crack at a near death experience for you because the first one wasn't as productive as you'd hoped. She doesn't have to say it. I can read it in the slump of her shoulders and the restlessness of her hands. She'll relent.

"I want to see if the changes stuck. If the gun's still where I put it. How much time has passed there since I blipped," I say. "Maybe he'll be home this time."

Those words cement her certainty. She nods slowly.

"I put the earring in my right pocket and now I can't reach it." I hold up my bandaged hand. "Do you mind?"

She smiles impishly. "Ah, I see. This is all a devious ploy to get my hand down your pants."

"How dare you question my perfectly innocent intentions," I say, thrusting my hips toward her with a lewd grin.

"Ugh. Stop," she says. I do because I'm tired and I made her smile and that's all I was after. She fishes the earring out of my pocket and places it in my left palm. "Come back to me whole."

"I'm not some soldier going off to war," I tease. "Thirty seconds. You won't even miss me."

She's suddenly serious again. "No more blood." She kisses my cheek.

"I'll try." I say, cradling my injured hand in my lap. "Be right back."

Chapter Sixteen

I go faster this time. I'm tired and that's taken the sharp edge off my fear. I've already weathered one panic attack and my body doesn't have the energy to launch into another, so I'm able to maintain a clear head when I blip into Adam's apartment this time.

I materialize in the living room again. Same spot. The bar of light has swung up onto the wall and I can't tell if I'm later in the same day or here on an entirely different one. I don't know how time works on these jumps. The room is empty, but the beer bottles on the counter have been cleared and the television remote is in a different spot. It was on the couch before and rests on the coffee table now.

Different day then? I listen for Adam's presence, but he's not here and I'm relieved and disappointed in turns. I wanted to do something concrete for Charlie, to interact with her brother and ensure he knows how much his sister loves him, how the hole that's eating him up inside, she feels it too. I want to tell him he's not crazy and that he's lucky to have her. He's the cornerstone of her whole world. But, deep down, I know I suck at talking to strangers, and I'm terrified of how Adam might respond to a ghost manifesting in his living room. The guy's not stable.

I don't waste time. Striding to the kitchenette, I crank open the cupboard under the sink and pull out a trash can. Cradling the bin carefully in my right arm, I use my left hand to shovel the block of butcher knives on the counter into it. I yank open drawers and scoop up every other knife I see within. Then I charge down the hallway to the bathroom and I empty everything in the medicine cabinet into the garbage. I make sure the nightstand drawer is empty. I've been scanning as I go, and I haven't seen anywhere he could hang himself. His ceilings are all smooth drywall, the shower head in the bathroom is too low and angles too sharply downward to use as an anchor point, and the curtain is held up by a tension rod. His closet doesn't have a bar to hang clothes on at all, just a rickety looking stand that wouldn't support weight, but I shove the hanger with all his ties clipped to it in the trash too, just in case.

There's no balcony outside and both of his windows have bars welded onto the interior to prevent jumping, like it's been a reoccurring problem in this building. I shudder at the thought.

I know I'm probably missing something, but I don't have time to clear out more. I leave Adam's apartment and the floor is still hard. Triumph spikes through me when I open the fire hose cabinet, still smeared with my blood, and find Adam's revolver tucked between the folds. I shove it in the bin with the rest of Adam's things and take the stairs as fast as I can. Out the complex's exit toward the closest alley.

The world wobbles and I crash into the building's wall as the pavement in the alley folds in and the darkness snaps at me. I make it to the garbage dumpster. The satisfying hollow clang of Adam's trash can hitting the bottom of the bin echoes through my head as the blackness hauls me under. An odd, hard smile twitches my lips as it does. I did it. I held it back longer this time.

Charlie is on the other side of the darkness, like she always is. She's holding my head in her lap when I come back to her. Her hand is on my chest, and my heart is thrashing like it's about to burst out of me. I'm clawing at my throat. My heels drum against the metal floor as my legs spasm, but every gulp of air clears my head, and her voice in my ears is home. When I can speak, I pant, "Cleared ... the whole apartment. He's not there, but anything h-he could hurt himself with, it's gone. The changes stuck, Charlie."

She looks down at me, eyes bright with tears.

"The gun was still where I hid it. I took it all. Bought us some time."

Her shoulders shake, and she curls over me as she cries, tears dripping onto my chest. My limbs feel too heavy to lift, but I groan and wrap an arm around her, pulling her against my sweaty chest. "It's okay," I murmur into her ear as our heavy breathing fills the room and we come down from terror.

"Thank you," she sobs.

"Anything for you, Charlie," I whisper. This is the closest I've felt to anyone in my entire life. Including my family.

God, I don't know if I'll be strong enough to leave her when the time comes.

We leave the truck at dawn. Charlie sets out her solar panels like she always does, but they aren't charging the battery packs properly and she can't figure out why. Even if we can endure the worsening headaches, we won't be able to stay up-tree if we can't maintain our batteries and keep up a safe zone of light at night. This world was supposed to be empty—so was the one that took Riley's leg. We can't take chances.

It's sunny today, so we scour the abandoned world further out, trying to find something to eat, but we don't have any luck. There're a few orphaned cans of pickled green beans at a corner grocery store, but the tins are swollen and neither of us has the slightest interest in contracting botulism from something as uninviting as green beans.

It's inevitable. Hunger rules us. We eventually surrender to it and go back to Charlie's safe world, but as soon as we cross the bridge, her disc tablet lets out a distressed beep, and her eyes widen. "Shit." She pulls out her keystone detector. "They're here."

"The Embassy?" I lean toward her. Four keystones blink in the northwest quadrant of the detectors compass. "How close?" Right as I say it, the resonance of tickets that aren't ours fills my ears. And then a freakish, dissonant howl. It's unmistakable and instantly petrifying. I've never heard it in a populated dimension.

A maneater.

The hair raises on my arms and my mouth dries out.

A cacophony down the block pulls at our attention and I see them. Six armed men in military uniform each one gripping a black lead clipped to a collared creature that is the most monstrous thing I've ever seen in my life.

Even from this distance, its skin looks sunburned badly. Layers of it blister and peel off in strips. All four of its spidery legs have been amputated above the elbows and knees, but that doesn't prevent the creature from lunging ahead on half-healed stumps, scrabbling for purchase on the sidewalk and leaving streaks of blood in its wake. The branched sail on its spine has been hacked off as well. Despite the ghastly injuries, it's locked onto our position, skull sockets like black holes, bloodied toothless jaw snapping as it snarls and screams and yanks the men holding it back toward us.

That's when I realize that the soldiers aren't holding leads. The maneater isn't wearing a collar. Instead, the men are holding braided cables of IDOCS. A network of them stabs under the skin of the creature's neck and spine. They've hijacked its nervous system and are yanking on lines to control it like a puppet. Even maimed and hobbled, the alien creature is terrifyingly strong. It bowls over pedestrians on the sidewalk. Several people, blind to its reckless charge, crash against buildings or ricochet into the street.

Horror jabs through me as brakes screech, and a car veers to avoid an older man who fell into its path. Onlookers shriek as the front tire rolls over his back like a pizza cutter slicing through dough. His legs go limp as he snags on the vehicle's undercarriage.

Oh my God.

Charlie grabs my arm, pulls me back into the Toyota Corolla. We tumble back to the abandoned world.

"What was that?" I yell at her back as she starts sprinting toward the mall.

She doesn't answer.

"Charlie, what the hell was that thing?"

"Ticket tracker," she calls over her shoulder, voice thin and trembling. "We need to move."

It hits me all at once, as I'm loping behind her sick and flushed with fresh adrenaline. "The Embassy uses maneaters?"

"Incapacitated ones."

Incapacitated. Jesus Christ, they mutilated it, cut off its legs, ripped out its connection to the rest of its horde, pulled out its teeth. "Y-you said there weren't any maneaters on Prime."

"Not from Prime. They keep them in a garage world. Here." Charlie tosses something back and I instinctively raise my hand to catch it.

The buzzing in my ears crescendos. I look down at a house key. A ticket.

"We need to split up," she says. "Throw the tracker off in case it gets through." She grabs another ticket from the orange pouch, skids to a stop at an intersection and hurls the object down a side street. A grocery cart token pings as it bounces off the pavement.

Cold fear picks at my stomach. "Charlie those are our tickets to get back!"

"Not if that thing finds us. Go. That way." She points down the opposite street. "Drop the key somewhere then circle back and meet me at the truck."

I do what I'm told, running until my lungs sting and stitches lance below my ribs. Then, I drop the house key down a storm drain.

I can't get the image out of my head, the sunburned maneater charging toward us like a bloodied harpooned whale. God, I hope it can't get through.

Our trackers haven't materialized by the time I get to the armored truck. Charlie jams equipment into duffle bags while I collapse the tripods that hold our lights. She tucks the orange ticket pouch into the zippered travel bag under her shirt and shoves the AED into her duffle bag. We throw everything over our shoulders and flee, leaving a mess of sleeping bags in our wake.

"You have any other tickets?" I puff as we run. The ringing that's filled my head since we started this trip has muted significantly. Shit. She's tossed almost all of them, hasn't she?

"No. We just need some distance. Come on."

Adrenaline only fuels me so far. I tire and slow, lagging behind Charlie. She's stronger than I am. Hasn't fallen on her head several times in the past few days. That likely helps. She slows, lets me catch up. "Where are we going?" I ask.

"We need to get to an alternate gateway so they can't corner us here."

"You know where one is?" I ask hopefully.

"No. I kept the car keys though. We'll find another Corolla. Draw the Embassy retrievers over the bridge toward us. Out of my world. Then we can hopscotch back over and get lost in the tree before they catch us. The dark walker must have been too big to fit in the damned car or their ticket isn't working, otherwise they'd be here by now. We can slow down. Take a breath."

We walk for hours, weaving through parkades with Charlie keeping an eye on her keystone detector. The Embassy never materializes. The dismembered maneater doesn't either. We've walked somewhere close to twenty kilometers and it's an hour before sunset when we finally find what we're looking for. By then, we're starving. Our feet are blistered and throbbing when I see the swooping oval of a Toyota emblem on the trunk of a black sedan parked in front of a hair salon.

"Charlie?" I breathe.

Her gaze lifts from her tablet and she follows my line of sight. "Holy shit. Is it..."

I cross the street, squinting at the lettering above the taillight on the right side. Laughter bursts out of me. "Corolla. Jesus, I've never been so happy to see a car in my life. Check it?"

She grins, dropping her duffle bag between us, and handing me the almost empty orange pouch before opening the driver's side door. The keys don't fit in the ignition all the way, but it doesn't matter. As soon as Charlie reaches for the door handle, she's gone.

"It works!" she says breathlessly when she gets back.

"Now what?"

"We wait. Draw them over." She shoulders her bag and nods at the sun dipping below the buildings to the west. "If they're coming through, they'll do it within the next hour. They won't risk crossing in the dark. Sunlight weakens a tracker, but it'll be too strong for its handlers at night. They'll have to cage it up until sunrise. Let's get inside and set up."

The hair salon is in a bay with large, dusty windows. Nothing's stirring within. The front door is locked and when we break the glass to gain entry, we don't hear anything shifting in the storage area of the building. Charlie unholsters her weapon and searches the space while I stand beside a row of barber's chairs. The air still holds hints of astringent perm solution. Scissors and combs sit in dried out disinfectant jars. Razors and clips are lined up in trays with surgical precision. Sun bleached posters of intense men and women with high fashion hairstyles glare at me from the walls. Someone's family picture curls where it's been tucked into the frame of a mirror with the name *Marlene* written in what looks like lipstick. Shelves of hair spray, mousse, pomade, and God knows what else collect dust along the walls.

"Clear," Charlie yells and I sigh and follow the sound of her voice into what used to be a break room. It's got a solid lockable door and enough floorspace to sleep on.

It won't be enough, the defeatist in me insists. *They're coming for us. They'll trap us in here and it's not just one maneater this time. It's guys with guns.*

Sunset blazes orange under the crack in the door and then fades.

Charlie is quiet. When she finally takes her eyes off her keystone detector, I say "Give me the earring, please."

She'd asked for it back last night and I'd handed it over, watching as she removed her intact earring and tucked it alongside the one with the lost fastener into the travel pouch like they were the tiniest of security blankets. As we'd walked today, she'd brushed her earlobes more times than I could count, missing them.

Missing him.

"Now?" Charlie tries to sound annoyed, but I can see it in her face. Fragile hope. A desperate need to fix the mess she's made with Adam before the Embassy comes for us and we run again.

And I know this is my last chance to repay her for saving my life, to show her that I keep my promises. I fire her a cocky grin that I most certainly don't feel, and I hold my hand out. "Third time's the charm," I say.

She gives me the earring.

I'm getting more practiced. I blip into Adam's apartment easily this time.

And I'm right. The third time is the charm.

Charlie's brother is here with me.

He sits on the couch with a slack look on his face, and a gun in his lap.

Chapter Seventeen

Adam doesn't startle like I expect him to. I know he sees me because his gaze snaps to my face and stays there. He squints and cocks his head. The sunlight blazing through the window makes the blond stubble on his jawline look like translucent specks of gold. He wears a lilac-coloured dress shirt and a black tie. His suit jacket is neatly folded on the couch beside him.

Everything about this seems off. Wrong. What's he doing home midday dressed for work? And why in the hell is he so casual about me materializing in his living room? How did he find the gun?

It's not the same weapon, I realize as he brings it up to his face and scratches his cheek with the barrel. The one I got rid of was a revolver and this one looks like an automatic pistol.

He bought another gun, you idiot. Did you honestly think you could stop him by child-proofing his freaking apartment? As the thought crashes into me, Adam hoists the weapon and aims it at my chest.

"You're not real." His voice sounds rusty, like he hasn't spoken in a hundred years.

"No need to point a fucking gun then, is there?" I wince at my impulsive words.

"Touché." A joyless laugh puffs out of him, but he doesn't lower the pistol.

I show him my palms. "You often see people who aren't real, Adam?"

"When I was young." He doesn't question how I know his name. If he thinks I'm some sort of hallucination, a manufactured extension of himself, the devil on his proverbial shoulder, then I guess my familiarity with him would be the least shocking part of all this.

I take in his red-rimmed eyes, pale hair as white as corn silk, a beer bottle cradled between his legs. He looks like someone who carefully coiffed, ironed, and buttoned up to meet a day that crushed him under its heel. "A sister? Is that who you saw?"

Anger snarls up Adam's face. He jerks forward and the bottle jiggles and sloshes beer onto his pressed pants. Baring his teeth, he growls "Fuck off." The vitriol in his words makes me back up a step.

I try a different tack. "You ever see anyone else ... not real?"

"Who knows." He plucks up the beer and takes a loud swallow, all the while still aiming the gun steadily in my direction. "Hard to tell who's real anymore and who isn't."

I'm getting pulled from here, but it's not the darkness. Not yet. Memory clutches me into its cold talons and jerks me back to the parking lot behind the Dairy Queen where Sam Ren's lackeys beat the piss out of me, where he held a gun to my head. At the time, it'd been the most surreal moment of my life. Now, it seemed like a recollection belonging to someone else. Another life. Another branch of myself.

Adam doesn't exude glacial evil like Sam did, but there's a calm resignation about him that's equally petrifying, like he's spent all day getting used to the feel of this new gun in his hand and now it's an extension of him. I breathe against the stiffness in my chest and say, "I'm real, Adam. Why would you imagine me? Look, I busted my fingernail off." I hold up my bandaged finger and the action makes it throb angrily. "And I've got a bruise on my cheek. You wouldn't include details like that if you made me up, would you?"

"Dunno." He shrugs, but his brow creases, and he lowers the gun.

His next words come out with all the weight of a parishioner confessing sins. "I'm not right in the head."

"You're right enough to know when someone's been messing around in your apartment. Things have gone missing recently, haven't they? If I'm not real, how did I take your gun and all your sharp knives?"

His eyes narrow. "That was you, fucker?"

Tread carefully. Don't mess this up. "Yeah, that was me. I'm real and so is Charlie. She's worried about you. No matter what this world is trying to tell you, no matter how much it erases her, deep down, you know she's real."

Adam goes rigid again at the mention of her. The air twists around him, humming like guitar strings cranked too tight, and I know I've overstepped. I'm certain he's going to raise the gun and put me down when, suddenly, tension bleeds out of his shoulders and his face crumples. His eyes go glassy with tears, and he blinks up at the ceiling before taking a shuddering breath.

"I remember the first night she came. She was so small the bottom bunk just swallowed her up. She cried like a lost thing. It felt wrong lying in the bed above her, listening to that. I was too young to know how to fix it, so I just passed down my teddy bear. Sometime in the night, she ripped the limbs off it, pulled out all its stuffing. Picked off its eyes. She was strong for a such little thing. When I found it the next morning and asked her why she did it, you know what she said?"

I shake my head, unable to grasp where he's going with this.

"Barely a year old and clear as day she said, 'Wanted it.' Brown eyes, big and innocent. Already sucking me in. She didn't have anything of her own yet, so she tore it apart because in her mind, that was better than someone taking it away from her. I sewed it up, gave it back to her all patched up, and told her it was hers. A present. But the next time she got sick or scared or sad at night, she tore that bear to pieces, like it was a dog toy. It got to the point where I couldn't fix it anymore, so I saved up my allowance and bought her a new one. Even then, she never believed it was something she could keep."

He wipes his mouth and stares at the water-stained picture in the silver frame on his windowsill. "Why would I make that up? Why in the hell would everyone think I made her up? Samantha and Gene blamed me for ripping apart the bear. They thought it was odd that I kept stitching it back up afterward. And then when Charlie disappeared, I went crazy, and they couldn't help. Samantha never was much good at helping. If it can't be fixed with a sunshine-up-your-ass quote cross-stitched onto a pillow, she doesn't know how to cope. So, her and Gene put me in therapy. For years. *Years.* Shrinks told them that I manifested my sister because I had problems connecting socially. They tried to brainwash it into me, that she'd never been real. She was just some elaborate imaginary friend and I needed to grow up." A sharp laugh bursts out of him. "You know, for a long time, I thought they killed her. That maybe that's what they did with foster kids who didn't work out. I was convinced that Samantha and Gene were murderers, and the shrinks were colluding with them, that they'd buried her somewhere and turned the whole world against me because I wouldn't play nice and forget her."

"She hasn't forgotten you," I say gently. "She didn't come from here, so she couldn't stay. She wanted to, but this world made her too sick."

"She was sick a lot," he confirms.

"She had to go home, but she wants more than anything to come back. She loves you."

His voice goes flat. Dark. "Charlie doesn't know how to love."

"She does."

"Yeah? Then, how come you're here and she's not?"

"I'm helping. She's gotten in trouble for coming back. People in our world are hunting her down. I found a way to skip from our world to yours without raising any alarm bells, but it's dangerous, so I came alone. I left her just now, so I can tell her anything you want when I go back."

"And how do I know you aren't ... something else?" He pins me with a hard, desperate stare, and I recognize something in him. A commonality. A kinship. He's seen the darkness too. It's brushed against him in his nightmares, whispered horrible things, beckoned him toward death. Maybe he can sense it on me, the smell of hot iron, black smoke, and deep cold.

"An angel?" I try to steer the subject casually.

A humourless smile cracks his face. "Darker than that."

"I look so threatening?" I try for a goofy grin and fail. The tension in the room rises. It's making my neck itch.

"Sure as hell don't look holy," Adam answers.

I glance at the gun in his hand. "Do you believe in the afterlife?"

He looks down too. Swallows hard. Shakes his head. "There's other places. Other worlds—Charlie's proof of that much. But after we die? No. Nothing after that. We're just specks of life that crawled out of the black. Mistakes. Chaotic evolution that went too far and thinks too highly of itself. Look at us. We're hardly here to begin with. Just electrons and protons clinging to impossible organization, all waiting to come apart again. Some of us aren't put together right in the first place, and we can feel it, can't we?" He looks back up, his eyes hollow wells. "The *wrongness* of us. How all our empty spots are trying to collapse even as we fight our way through life. No, there's no afterlife. When we're gone, there's nothing but the blackness we crawled out of swallowing us back up." The tired relief in his voice sends ice down my spine.

"You and her like cinnamon candy," I blurt, fighting the cold resignation in him with something warm. "Not the hard ones that cut up your tongue—the soft ones like jellybeans."

"Hot Tamales." He winces at the memory.

"You used to play a game to see who could stuff the most in their mouth without spitting them out."

His laugh sounds like a sob. "She always won. Stubborn as hell. You do know her then."

"I do." I smile back, but my heart starts to squeeze in my chest. I feel like I'm swimming in deep water and can't see down, but I can sense something ascending with slow, primal strength. The darkness. *Goddamnit. Not yet.* I need to convince Adam to live, so I pull Charlie's pearl earring from my pocket, and I set it on the coffee table between us.

It rolls back and forth, a tiny pendulum on the polished surface.

His eyes go wide, and he makes a choking sound deep in his throat. "It was her. I knew it." I must look confused because he adds, "She came back, my last year of high school. Pretending to be someone else, but she reminded me so much of Charlie, I knew it wasn't a coincidence. And I wanted her to stay, so I pretended too. Played the part she wanted me to. I found the earrings at a second-hand store, and I gave them to her when we went out for supper one night. She laughed. Said pearls were a gift for an old woman, but I told her they reminded me of her. Oysters wrap themselves up in hardness to protect all their soft bits. She disappeared not long after that. Can't believe she kept them."

"I've never seen her without them." I lick my lips, feet rooted to the floor, afraid that if I move too fast or speak too loudly, the blackness will swallow me before I'm done. "Listen, she wants you to be happy. She's worried sick about you. She loves you and she's trying to find her way back here, but she can't come yet."

His eyes are changing, like he can sense the darkness crowding around both of us now. There's something unhinged in his voice when he asks, "You can pass on a message for me?"

"I can."

Tearing his gaze away, he nods slowly like he's trying to gather strength. His fingers flex on the gun. "Tell her to stop."

"I'm sorry?" I frown.

"Tell her to stop coming. To stop leaving me reminders. I don't want to see her again. She lies. Hides herself behind layers and thinks that no-one can see through them. She's doing it to you right now. Showing you whatever version of herself she thinks will work best to get you to do what she wants. I don't even like Hot Tamales. I only ever ate them because the stupid game made her laugh, made her happy."

The floor's going soupy, the darkness toying with me. There's no urgency to it this time. If it's hungry, it's holding back, smug and certain of something. *This is wrong,* my mind blares. *Something's wrong. It's never taken me slowly like this.* "Look, Adam. I don't know much, but I know she loves you, more than anything. Don't do this. Please. She's fighting for you."

"She's pulling me apart," he sobs. "Every time she's here, I feel it. Even when I can't see her, I feel … thinner. Like atoms splitting. I can't live like this. I'm sick of pretending I want to."

"Do it for her then." The words taste like ash as soon as they come out of my mouth.

Adam gapes at me like I've transformed into something monstrous. "Everything I did was for her. *Everything,*" he says. "And she left. She keeps leaving. Tearing everything apart in her wake. She doesn't even know. She has no idea how to stitch things back together. Only how to rip them apart." He stands up.

My feet sink into the floor.

I don't look down, but he does.

His eyes bulge. "You're…" He blinks at the carpet lapping around my ankles. His next words hiss through his teeth. "You're not with her. You're with *it.*"

"Adam…" I hold my palms out. I can't step back. The floor sets like cement around my calves, the darkness holding me there.

"Did you bring it here to watch?" he asks quietly, chambering a round in the gun and aiming it at my chest.

"I didn't bring it," I choke. "It follows me. Pulls me back to the world I left."

Emotion drains from his face and drops out of his voice. "Back to her?"

I can't answer. My tongue feels dead in my mouth.

"Back to her?" he barks, and spittle sprays my face as he jams the gun against my sternum.

"Y-yes." My heart is going haywire in my chest, the sound of it muting everything else in the room. I barely hear Adam when he speaks next.

"Goddamnit." He breaks away, turning and grinding the heels of his hands to his temples. Sweat blotches the under arms of his dress shirt. His gun points aimlessly toward the ceiling as he paces.

Take it from him, my mind screams, but the darkness holds me firm, locked around my lower legs like a python. I can't feel my feet. *You can still stop this. Convince him.* "Adam, listen to me." My voice shakes. "Don't listen to it. Don't let it—"

"I won't let it get her too." He pivots and shoots me in the chest.

My ribcage shudders as the bullet punches through my lung and out between my shoulder blade and spine. The shockwave tears through me like I'm tissue paper. It's not the force that knocks me down, it's the shock. *Oh my God, he fucking shot me.* Air pounds out of me. Everything defaults to shut-down mode. I crumble backwards, my head thudding on the carpet before the pain even comes.

Adam crosses the space between us like an automaton, face dead, slender figure towering over me. He shoots again before I can react. The bullet hammers through me, on the right side, just above the first impact. I whimper, trying to inhale, but the twin holes in my chest make a sick sucking noise and I can't pull enough air in. My hands reach up to press against the wounds as blood bubbles past them. Pain skewers through me, hot and sizzling.

Adam jams the barrel of the gun into his mouth.

No, I try to say, but instead I cough blood.

He pulls the trigger.

Red mist jets out the back of his skull. Paints the ceiling. He tips forward. The floor vibrates as he lands hard beside me, muscles twitching, eyelids fluttering, mouth gulping air like a fish.

"Adam?" The word gurgles out of me.

His gaze swings toward me for a second, and then his eyes lose focus.

We lie on the carpet face to face.

A deep red pool haloes his head. Too much blood. It creeps toward me until it's touching my cheek.

He stops breathing.

The darkness laps at us both, slipping into the exit wounds on my back and fingering my insides, relishing my fear. The agony of it takes my breath away. Adrenaline tingles as it rushes through me, numbing the burning, convincing my body that it still has the strength to live. To escape. But that's a lie. I'm not strong enough to fight this. No-one is. The darkness pulls me under, even as it leaves the dead husk of Adam crumpled on his living room floor. And I feel that calmness I've been searching for the other times it took me, the stillness people settle into when they're dying.

I think about Charlie and how, in the blink of an eye, I've failed her. But as life drains out of me, my last thoughts are of my family. Of Dad. Of James.

Always James.

I hope he lives. I hope the darkness never finds him again.

Chapter Eighteen

My lungs burn like I've breathed in water instead of air. Someone's wailing, braced over me. I look down and see my shirt's been cut apart. Bloody hands press a thick dressing against my right upper chest. There's a pad stuck to the bare skin above it and another further down on the left side. Wire leads snake out of them. They're bloody too. Everything is.

Something beeps like a metronome.

An unearthly howl fills the room, shrill as metal sheering apart.

A massive weight crashes into the door, cracking wood.

"Wake up, David," the voice screams. "Wake up!"

I know that voice. I know her, but I can't stay.

A team of men with helmets and guns carry me in a reinforced fabric stretcher. I've only woken up because they're jarring the hell out of me. Trying to shove me into the back bench seat of a car, and I don't fit. Someone is crying hysterically, ripping AED pads off my chest without regard for the skin that peels off with them. I'm still bleeding out. I can't get enough air.

"We're not going through until you check his pockets."

"He's dying!"

"Standard protocol. No incidental keystones. You can check his pockets, or we can cut the rest of his clothes off." Someone hollers, but I can't stay.

The next time I wake up, I'm alone. I'm in a bed and my chest feels like someone took a sledgehammer to it. Curved plexiglass arcs overhead, scuffed with scratches. A 360-degree camera. Beyond that, rusted, industrial rafters. I cry like a baby when I realize where I am—and that hurts like a bitch, crying.

Hamster Ball.

The bed opposite me is empty, sheets stripped, mattress bare.

A conversation slices through my muddy brain.

"Charlie?"

"Yeah?"

"If you take me back there, I'll never see the outside of a hamster ball again. I'll be their guinea pig forever."

"Yeah."

Wailing, I try to rip the IDOCS out of my arm, but my wrists are restrained. So are my ankles. I'm alone in here. Cold drugs slither into me as the monitoring system reacts to my hiccupping breaths and jackhammering heart.

Sedatives.

I scream something wordless at the camera, but I can't stay.

I don't know how long the Embassy keeps me in limbo while I heal. Time is a funny thing on Prime. Even funnier in solitary confinement while heavily drugged. My first memories are like dreams, hazy and immaterial. I vaguely recall waking up the first time they free one of my hands. I claw the IDOCS out of my left wrist before using my teeth to rip out the one buried in my free arm, but I don't realize they're in my legs too until I feel cold fluid creeping up my veins. "Damn it," I wheeze too late to do anything else before the machine puts me under again.

The next time I regain consciousness, I'm fully restrained again. A big man I don't recognize sits in a folding chair inside the hamster ball with me, cradling a clipboard on his lap.

"You're still recovering," he says in an even voice. "I understand this must be disorienting, but we need to ask a few—"

He doesn't finish because I scream until the IDOCS sedate me again.

The blackness swallows me up.

It's not that I *want* to go to it. I'm not insane. Trust me, I'm just as motivated as the next guy to avoid circumstances that feel like tortuous death. It's just that being awake is too much right now. My mind keeps shutting down, and there's nowhere else to go once it does. The darkness is always there. Jaws yawning wide. Waiting.

The Embassy gets smarter. It's hard to interrogate somebody who keeps escaping into unconsciousness, so they take that avenue away from me.

The next time I come to, the IDOCS are gone and so are my restraints. I have to piss badly. Sitting up, desiccated and dizzy, I cling to the edge of the bed. For a few petrified moments, I'm horrified I'm going to fall, but then my head clears, and even though my body feels a hundred years old, I lock my knees and stand. The acrylic floor is cold against my bare feet. It hums with the reverberations of hidden machinery beneath. I hang onto the edge of the cot, shuffle to the wall, and lean on the plexiglass all the way to the stainless-steel bathroom vestibule. My balance is way off, but I manage to aim and hit the toilet.

After I shiver and shake off, I catch my reflection in the safety mirror.

I'm rail thin, arms covered in Band-Aids at the IDOCS entry points. I look like a walking cadaver. Someone's shaved my face while I slept—a creepy-as-hell thought in itself—and they missed a spot just below my jaw. A synthetic, backless gown hangs off me, the same kind I wore when I first woke up in quarantine with Charlie. It hurts to reach back, but I manage to pick apart the ties at my neck. I close the accordion door, even though it's likely there's a hidden camera to monitor my movements in here too. Then, I shrug out of the hospital gown.

Unease creeps like frost up my spine as I stare at my chest. A red oval of a scar, smaller than the end of my finger divots the pale skin in between my sternum and nipple. There's another one higher up, closer to my collarbone. I run a finger over both. The wounds feel numb. So do I. None of this seems real. Turning, I angle to see my back. It aches when I do. The right side of my ribcage feels like it's only held together by cobwebs of scar tissue. One exit wound scar puckers frighteningly close to my spine. The other one is bigger and below my shoulder blade. Fresh IDOCS scabs around it suggest a more recent reparative operation. Anxiety grips me. *How long have I been out if everything's healed so much already?*

As I lean down to pick up the discarded hospital gown, dizziness pounces. It eats at the edges of my vision and sending me crashing against the accordion door, which rattles loudly but holds as I find my balance.

Somewhere outside, an intercom crackles loudly, startling me. "Please come out of the lavatory, Mr. Enril."

I laugh. I can't help it. The ridiculousness of all this, the formality of the request, the warning pain in my ribs, it all hits me at once. Suddenly, I'm drowning in the memory of bullets vibrating like bees as they sliced through me. Adam standing over me while I squirmed, inhumanly tall. The splatter of blood and brain matter like some bold piece of modern art on his white ceiling. "In a minute," I gasp, suddenly unable to draw breath.

"Mr. Enril, you have thirty seconds to comply before we lower the oxygen levels and render you unconscious."

"Jesus Christ. Coming." *No camera in the bathroom, then.* A detached, analytical part of my mind announces through the chaotic flash-back. *Not if they're antsy when they hear a crash in here.*

The voice on the intercom is counting down single digits by the time I come back to myself enough to gingerly scoop up the hospital gown and ease into it. Wrestling the accordion door open, I make my way back to the bed, exhausted by the short trek. I lie down without pulling the blankets up and almost instantly fall asleep.

The next time I wake up, the guy in the folding chair is back again. Just … sitting there.

"They pay you to watch me sleep?" My voice is groggy.

"Not enough," he answers evenly, sliding a pen off his clipboard with a sigh, like we're starting a job interview and I've showed up late and underdressed.

"Are you ready to cooperate, Mr. Enril?" He looks like military, or hired muscle, sharp and rough, but his voice is so at odds with the rest of him. It's patient, a bit patronizing, like he's some sort of royalty trying to tone down an elitist accent and failing miserably.

"I've got to piss." I swing my legs out of the bed and shuffle past him to the bathroom cubicle. And I make damned sure to take my time, avoiding my haggard reflection, washing my hands like I'm a doctor prepping for a surgery, taking several long slurps from the faucet because I'm thirsty as hell and no-one has offered me anything to eat or drink. I'd loiter for longer, but my legs feel like overcooked noodles. I'm scared that I'll collapse in here and have to ask for help.

And I don't want to owe any favours to the Duke of Dickwad out there.

I brace myself to face him. Then, I make my way back to the bed only slightly out of breath. It takes everything I have to stay sitting up when I get there.

The guy's tall. He'd tower over me if he were standing, but he doesn't need stature to intimidate. A severe brush cut, broad shoulders and well-muscled arms are a quiet proclamation that he's not the type to be trifled with. "We have questions we need answered," he says and somehow, his soft tone makes it sound like a threat.

My guard goes up, and I swallow against heat. "Me too," I say. "Where's Charlie?"

"We'll get to that if you provide us some insight as to how exactly you've been travelling interdimensionally without using bridges or experiencing the effects of time dilation."

I'm in no shape to puff out my chest and play tough, but I'm tired. And pissy. It's a bad mix. "I think we'll get to it now, or we're done," I snap.

Nothing in his expression changes. He uncrosses his legs and the chair creaks as he leans forward. He doesn't raise his voice. "Do you have any idea how many ways we can hurt you, Mr. Enril?"

I lean forward too, even though fear is boiling through me, and I'm pretty sure this guy's about to knock me into next week. "Fuck. Off."

He nods. Stands. A quick glance at the overhead camera is the only signal he uses to prompt the hamster ball walls to roll upward, revealing the exit port. My stomach sinks, already expecting the fall when the port seals behind him and he announces casually, "Drop the oxygen levels."

Something hisses through the air vents.

"Shit." I stand, smack my palms against the plexiglass. "Don't! Please." But he's already walking away.

Exhaustion settles over me like a wet blanket. A giddy feeling slips through me as I slide down to the floor, but there's nothing after that. Nothing but the black.

I'm starting to get used to it. That's messed up right? I'm starting to get used to the darkness. To feeling like I'm dying.

A tension headache squeezes my skull. My stomach cramps with hunger, so I drink water from the bathroom tap until I hear it sloshing around whenever I move. I pace, stretch, and take deep breaths because I remember having pneumonia as a kid, and Mom telling me that stretching my lungs was important while they were healing.

Embassy employees in lab coats string cable outside of the hamster ball, neatly ignoring me as they set up four more cameras on tripods. I'm a movie star now, I guess?

The Duke of Dickwad comes back every few hours, ensuring I can't get a decent stretch of sleep, and we settle into a stubborn stalemate. I ask him about Charlie. He doesn't answer. He asks me about my newfound dimension-hopping abilities. I tell him to where he can shove his clipboard, at which point, he leaves and has my air supply cut off.

They starve me too. Just enough to make me miserable. I haven't been offered a solid meal since I've been imprisoned, but I've woken up on the floor with a raw throat and an IDOCS retreating away from me enough times to know that my captors have been inserting a feeding tube to keep me alive. The Embassy doesn't want me dead. They just want to wear me down until I crack.

One day, the oxygen levels drop in the hamster ball while I'm alone. I make it back to the bed before I slump over and, when I wake up, I'm restrained. The straps at my wrists and ankles dig in tightly enough that my fingers and toes are cold and throbbing.

And the duke is in the room.

Without his clipboard.

Instead, he holds a tray of nasty-looking stainless steel surgical tools. Mostly variations of pliers. "I didn't want it to come to this," he says.

Oh, Jesus. My heart kicks into overdrive and my mouth dries out. A small laugh puffs out of me, the inappropriate, nervous kind. "Oh, I don't know. You seem the type that gets off on this sort of thing."

"Teenage cheek isn't going to save you, Mr. Enril. We need to know how you operate, and my superiors are getting impatient."

"I'd hate for you to get a bad performance review."

The duke sets the tray on the floor and plucks up a pair of pliers. He grabs my right hand.

Breath hisses between my teeth as I jerk away from him, but the restraints bite in, and I can't move. He pries my middle finger up and sets the jaw of the pliers under the corner of the fingernail.

I expect it to go fast, like in the movies, like when I tore my index fingernail off when I fell in the hallway outside Adam's apartment. Quick, brutal, and shocking.

But the duke doesn't go quickly. He peels the corner of my nail upward with excruciating slow precision.

I try to muffle my wail, but it's impossible. I'm screaming within seconds.

"Tell me how you travelled without a gate, how you bypassed time dilation," he shouts over my cries. The nail bends and starts to peel up like a label coming away from a jar.

"I don't know!" I screech. "Please, I don't know."

He jiggles the plier jaw under the middle of my nail and starts prying there. "You did it more than once, Mr. Enril. We have witnesses."

I'm thrashing on the mattress, so overcome by pain that I can't talk, can't inhale, so he pauses.

Every breath is a sob. Blood runs down my finger, warming the back of my hand.

"Be reasonable. We're only asking for your cooperation. You owe us, after all. We saved your life, Mr. Enril. You would have died without numerous intricate—and quite expensive—surgeries. Answer one question for me, and we'll stop for today."

I nod, hand trembling.

"Did you travel without a ticket?"

"No ticket," I gulp.

He tugs the nail upward.

"NO TICKET!" I howl. "Please stop. Pleasestop. Oh, God."

"Did you travel without a bridge?"

"N-no bridge. Keystone. I used a keystone."

"Impossible." He murmurs and pries harder.

And in that moment of delirious pain, I realize, he's not going to stop. This isn't going to stop, and I've got eighteen more nails he can rip out. He's proficient enough at this, he won't let me lose consciousness. He'll make it last forever. It pushes me over the edge. My cries twist into hysterical laughs.

The duke frowns and wrenches harder. I barely hear his words over the roar in my head. "Where do you go?" he asks.

My whole world snaps, like tension cables twisted too tight. Fear, pain, anger, frustration, all rupture out of me. "Where do I go?" I roar, bucking off the table toward him hard enough that he flinches. "Fuck you! You think you can hurt me? You think you can do worse than the darkness? Where do I *go*? Somewhere that feels like dying over and over again. You think you can beat that? Fuck you." I spit. "FUCK. YOU! WHERE'S CHARLIE?"

He rips the nail off cleanly and I don't even feel it.

Then he leaves. He doesn't take the tray. The hamster ball walls rumble and rotate upward, and when the duke is gone, all that's left is the *plip plip plip* of my blood dripping onto the hard floor, and all my fire draining out along with it, leaving me cold and shaking.

I cry. I don't care that the cameras are watching me. I cry until I can't breathe.

I'm never going home. I'm going to die in here alone.

Chapter Nineteen

I wake up to the smell of disinfectant and a bandaged middle finger that feels like it's been ground into hamburger. My ankle and wrist restraints are off, the tray of pliers is gone, and the floor is squeaky clean. I wonder—not for the first time—how many oxygen shortages a person can suffer before it causes permanent damage.

The next time someone comes to visit, the Embassy doesn't bother to knock me out first. They let me see him coming as he breaches the tarped-in cubicle surrounding my enclosure.

"Cory," I breathe as I recognize the big man.

He has a bowl in his hand and a folded tv tray tucked under one arm. He ducks under the portal as it's still yawning open. I'm not ready for the wave of nostalgia seeing him triggers. It snarls up my stomach and squeezes air out of my lungs. God, I've missed him. I didn't realize how much until now.

"Hey kid. Hold this?" He passes me the bowl, and I grab it with both hands. It's full of steaming chicken broth. The smell of it makes my mouth water and my stomach cramp.

Cory sets up the tv tray and pats it once with a big hand. "There." The portal disappears into the floor behind him, and I stand staring dumbly.

His face is creased. His cheeks look hollowed out, but he still looks like wise mentor from all my childhood movies. "You're older," I blurt.

"No shit. You don't look so hot yourself."

"They send you in here to be the good cop?" My hands are shaking, jiggling the warm bowl. I don't want to let it go, but food seems like a trap, so I set it down on the tv tray hard enough that it sloshes.

"Something like that," he says, pulling a set of cutlery rolled in a napkin from his chest pocket. When I stand there frozen, he shrugs, steps away from me, and leans back against the plexiglass wall. "Might as well eat first. You look as used up as a hooker after a Friday night in the Pot."

I fumble with the cutlery. The spoon dribbles as I bring the first sip to my lips. And Goddamn, I swear, it's the best thing I've ever tasted. Like *ever.* It's salty, with undertones of garlic and celery, and it eases the stinging in my throat. I spill half the next spoonful, but I don't care. My next few moments distill down to shovelling as much of this rapture-in-a-bowl down my throat as I can before someone takes it away.

"Breathe every now and then, yeah?" Cory admonishes softly. "Jesus, they really did a number on you, didn't they?"

I slap down the spoon and gulp the soup straight out of the bowl. Broth dribbles down my chin and I wipe it away. When I'm done, I back away from Cory until my shoulder blades are pressing against the bathroom door because every part of me wants to hug the man and I don't trust that, don't like how the Embassy is using him to try and soften me up. "How much time since the grocery store parking lot?" I ask.

"When your girl shot me? Been about a year down here, give or take. Have they fed you at all?"

"No. How's Lee?"

That question shocks him. I can tell by how his eyebrows pop up and the way he clears his throat. "Lee is … in an institution. He's having a hard time."

"An institution like this?" I sneer nodding to the walls around us.

"Somewhere nicer. They let me visit him, and sometimes he remembers me." The big man's voice is the softest I've ever heard it. He scratches at the start of a beard that's greyer than I remember and then he sighs. "Why didn't you just answer their questions, kid?"

I straighten and smile coldly. I must look like some wild, cornered thing, because Cory slides his hand behind his back, and I spot the warped reflection of a gun tucked into his belt in the plexiglass.

And suddenly, it's all I can do not to hyperventilate. My body is convinced I'm about to get shot again and I can barely cram the panic down.

Cory's astute enough to see what's happening. He takes his hand off his gun and holds his palms out.

It's a long time before I can speak. "They wouldn't answer me. Not one question. They wouldn't tell me about Charlie. And their interrogator's a Goddamned prick."

He chuckles. I don't realize how much I've missed that deep belly laugh until now. "Stan? Yeah, he's a real piece of work."

Stan? The Duke of Dickwad's name is Stan? Christ. I swallow and cradle my hand against my chest. "Where's Charlie?"

"How 'bout you sit down, kid." He points his chin toward the bed.

"How about you tell me where Charlie is?" I speak through my teeth.

"Fine. Fine. Jesus, don't get your balls in a twist." He pulls out a pack of cigarettes and throws a long look at the camera above us as he pinches a smoke between his lips and lights it. "Turn off the smoke detectors," he orders whoever is watching. Then to me, he says, "I'd offer you one, but they were pretty damned insistent that cigarettes are awful for collapsed lungs."

"Cory." I must sound desperate because he takes a long drag and nods resolutely, face tired as smoke jets out his nostrils.

"She's in a hamster ball, like you are. Different city."

My throat closes. I've guzzled down the soup too fast and now nausea flutters through my stomach. "Did they..." My voice cracks. It takes several breaths before I can try again. "Are they interrogating her?"

"She's got a letter on her record."

"A letter on her record?" I laugh at the absurdity of it. I'm getting my fingernails torn off meanwhile Charlie gets a sternly worded reprimand?

Cory doesn't laugh. "It's more serious than it sounds. She already has one letter on file. This is her second one. Any citizen that gets three becomes a keystone mule, so she's on her last strike, kid."

"What?" I gape. "No. No, that's not how it works. Charlie said that keystone mules are criminals. Bad ones. People who were going to get executed anyway."

"Did she, now? How about you wake up and use your head. Just how long do you think it took before our supply of heinous felons went and dried up? Meanwhile the demand for mules only increased, and the Embassy is nothing if not resourceful. They *make* criminals. Understand? Three strikes and we're out. Me. Your girl. Any of us. The higher-ups spout some half-baked propaganda so the general public can sleep at night, but mules aren't criminals. Haven't been for a long, long time. They're just unlucky fucks who crossed the Embassy. Charlie's on thin ice. One more wrong move, and she's dead." He stops and shakes his head.

I feel the colour draining out of me. This is who my captors are. People who resolutely believe that the ends justify the means. Oh, God and they've got Charlie.

"Sit down," Cory orders this time, voice softer, but unyielding.

I limp over to the bed and sit. He stays leaning against the wall, blowing cigarette smoke toward the exhaust vent. "She ever tell you what happened to her partner?"

"The one that died?" My numb mind struggles to follow the change in subject.

"Yeah, the one that died. He was in love with her. It happens. Stressful job. Adrenaline. Endorphins. Saving each other's lives over and over. You've felt it this last bit, I'd wager. Almost dying does a helluva good job of making you feel alive, so it's not uncommon for Gatekeeper partners to join up in more ways than one."

"Her past is none of my business." I break eye contact with him, blushing.

"Oh, I think it is," Cory retorts. "Wouldn't bring it up if I didn't. Don't get me wrong. Charlie's a good kid, David. She's got a good heart, but you don't survive up-tree as long as she has without a certain skillset, and hers seems to be using people."

"She didn't *use* me," I hiss.

"She probably didn't mean to, not to begin with. It just comes to her naturally. Her partner—Ivan. She tell you how he died?"

Ivan. She never even told me his name. My brow creases as I try to replay the conversation Charlie and I had while that shitty electric car took us away from the warehouse we'd quarantined in. It seemed like lifetimes ago. "They got swamped by maneaters and he was the primitus keystone. He died to break the bridge and stop them migrating over."

He scrubs his beard and mumbles, "Not entirely untrue. He was the primitus and a damned good one too. Always followed protocol. Charlie not so much. She's been known to smuggle black-market tickets up-tree. This particular time, while she was waiting for Ivan to clear a world, she went on a little side-quest to visit her brother. But it turns out someone sold her a rotten ticket."

"Rotten?" I ask.

"A ticket tied to an infested world, like the one that got Riley."

I have nightmares about him when I'm not having nightmares about Adam. The bone jutting out of his masticated amputated leg. The shape of his body under the sheets in the hotel room bed. I blink furiously and refocus on Cory.

"She got swamped by a horde," he says. "As much as walkers like devouring people, they crave tickets even more." Cory shrugs. "She saved herself by throwing them a bone. Gave them her ticket. One of them swallowed it, and then the whole lot of them spilled into the world she'd just left, screaming in the daylight, scrambling for shade. It's a major offense to infect a cleared world, but Charlie probably would have been okay if the weather had held. Her and Ivan could have systematically hunted down the horde as they split up and hid in pockets of shade, lured them out before any other walker groups sniffed out the bridge and crossed. It wasn't a huge group. Charlie figured maybe fifteen of them all together."

"What happened?" I ask even though I don't want to know.

Cory lifts his boot and crushes his cigarette against its sole. "A storm came in. Ivan came back, and he and Charlie got so busy exterminating the walkers, they didn't see the clouds boiling up from nothing—that's how she tells it anyway. When it blotted out the sun, the horde swamped Charlie. She was the reserve, still holding the ticket bag for Ivan. And a bunch of tickets strapped to you is one hell of a walker attractant. Ivan cranked on his light-pack and that bought the pair of them enough time to get back to their gate, shooting down the bastards as they went." He stops there, looking at me from beneath his eyebrows like he's gauging whether I'm strong enough to hear the next bit.

"And then?"

"And then their guns ran out of charge. Charlie was at the gate when two of the walkers latched on to Ivan's light pack and busted it. She had to cross without him. She couldn't let the horde get a hold of a pile of tickets that would lead them all the way back to Prime. So, she left him there, and the dark walkers ate him alive."

I shudder. "She didn't have any other choice."

"He did." Cory sniffs. "There wasn't any need to stay there and dispatch those walkers. It was a cleared world, but it was an empty one. The smart thing would have been to cut his losses and drag Charlie home. Make her face the music. A letter on your record is harsh, but her file was clean up until that point, and lost worlds happen. The Embassy's more concerned about keeping Prime safe than preserving anywhere else. They might have even let her off with a slap on the wrist. Ivan would have known that. But he didn't want Charlie to get in trouble. He stayed to dispatch a rogue horde with her. I don't know if she talked him into it, or he was just smitten enough that he wanted to clean up her mess. So, he covered for her, and he died for that. Later, Riley died for her too. Strikingly similar circumstances, weren't they?"

I feel sick. "That's not her fault. Why are you telling me this?"

"Because I don't know if she's worth all this, kid. Charlie does what she has to, to come out on top. She knows how to survive, and she's good at making people love her. Probably doesn't even know she's doing it. You, on the other hand, don't seem to value your own life at all. Stan was in here with all his wicked little tools, and you barely gave him shit for intel." He turns the cigarette butt in his fingers, examining it like he doesn't remember why it's in his hand.

"What's your point?" I snap.

Cory sighs, tired eyes meeting mine. "Unfortunately, you *did* give the Embassy something. Granted, they'd already guessed that you care about Charlie. But you've gone and showed them you care about her *more* than you care about yourself. She's the only one you've asked after this whole time. Even while they tortured you, you asked for her."

My stomach plunges. I cover my mouth and breathe hard through my nose. *Oh God. Oh shit. How could I have been so stupid?*

"They're not interested in your fingernails anymore, David," Cory says quietly. "They know how to hurt you now."

"They'll hurt her?" I choke.

He nods.

The world spins sickly. Impotent rage burns through me. Bile rises in my throat. "You're not the good cop."

"No. Just the bearer of bad news. The Embassy gets what they want. They always get what they want, kid."

I snarl my fists up in my sweaty hair and swear every curse word I can think of, but it does nothing to dull the raw fear that's stripping me down to my bones. "What do I do?" I ask.

"Cooperate, for a start." Cory says. "That's why they brought me here. They figured we were close enough that you'd listen to me. They want you to blip. They want to study you while you do it."

I lick my lips, trying desperately to wrest some sort of control back from this situation. "I can't just do it on command."

Instant ire hardens Cory's eyes, but he keeps his voice low and even. "That right? Funny, because Charlie already told them that you can, and that you've done it more than once for her."

Betrayal braids into the sour mix in my stomach. The knowledge that she's told them about me while I've been holding everything in at all costs, it stings in a surprisingly fierce way.

When the stunned silence stretches between us, Cory snorts and asks sharply "Do you have *any* idea how you've changed things, kid? The ripples you're making in your wake. Do you even know what they're doing out there, right now?"

"No, I'm sorry," I snap back, irrational anger loosening my tongue. "Seems I've been a bit out of the loop lately with them constantly dropping the O_2 in here to keep me brain dead. So, enlighten me, Cory. What's been going on *out there* that's so damned important for me to know, huh?"

"I don't believe this." He pushes off the wall and stabs a finger at my chest. "You're the Embassy's fucking *golden boy* and you don't have a goddamned clue," he growls. "Ever since they first got you in a bubble, you know what they've been doing? Trying to *replicate* you. Do you have the slightest idea what that entails?"

I shake my head, arrogance bleeding out of me as fast as it filled me.

"Do you know how many tickets they've broken, how many shattered relics they've shoved down people's throats, trying to reproduce what you did?" His voice drops. "How many innocent people they've killed that way? And when that didn't work, when Charlie and you and I were all up-tree together, the Embassy didn't just twiddle their thumbs waiting for you to come back. No, they had months to play. *Months.* Do you know how many babies they sent to safe worlds with absolutely no intention of bringing them back when they get sick? They're just letting them die out there in foster worlds now. That's how it works since you came, David. Parents send their kids off, thinking they'll be safe and the Embassy just uses them as guinea pigs, playing the odds, watching to see if any of those poor little shits survives as long as you did, because they don't know what the magic factor is, what exactly made you so *special*, if it's the broken ticket, or the time you spent away from here, or the offshoot world, so they're trying it all. Shotgun science. *Killing babies*, David, because they want to replicate you."

"Oh, Jesus." I'm slipping away. The room feels colder.

"Yesterday, you went and told Stan you needed a keystone to blip. Do you know what the Embassy did with that little gem of information? How many mules they rounded up first thing this morning to go fetch keystones from dimensions they have a vested interest in? How many people they shot in the head when they returned this afternoon, just so you can have a ready supply of *dead* keystones to flit to any dimension you damned well please without the danger of reinforced bridges?"

I gag, but Cory doesn't let up.

"Maneaters can't blip. No-one in the universe can yet. Except you,

Golden Boy. You're the ace up their sleeve. Their nuclear weapon in a centuries-long, universe-wide cold war, a gatekeeper who doesn't even need a damned gate, who can travel without time dilation affecting them, and you don't think they know exactly how to use you? How to use all of *us* to use you?" His voice breaks, brittle with raw anger and fear.

An awful thought amidst all the other awful thoughts strikes me. *What if Lee didn't get sick?* What if the Embassy made him that way and then made sure he couldn't recover because that's how they keep Cory under their thumb?

Ringing squeals in my ears. My chest aches, my injured hand pounds, and my mind is flipping switches and pulling plugs on every emotion I have.

Cory says something I don't hear and then fishes an object out of his back pocket.

I flinch, terrified it's going to be some other implement of torture, but when I recognize it, it's worse. So much worse.

My lungs stick together like fly paper. Tears blur my vision.

And, I know, in this moment, that I'm the most selfish piece of shit in the whole universe.

Because the thing that pushes me over the edge and crushes me is not the staggering fact that the Embassy is experimenting on people, or condemning thousands of innocents to death as mules, or shipping orphaned babies to lonely worlds to die sick and alone because of me. It's not those world-shattering revelations that break me.

It's this.

This one small thing that doesn't affect anyone other than me.

This self-centred loss.

"Where did you find that?" I rasp.

"In Charlie's things. She said she was keeping it safe for you. They'll let you make one jump with it now, but then you have to give it back. If you play nice and do exactly what you're told, they won't hurt her, and they'll let you blip where you like as often as once a week. Understand?"

I can't answer, so I nod. When Cory holds it out, I take Everett's tobacco tin in my trembling fingers.

I never lost it. I never...

She took it.

Charlie.

She took it, stole it from me while I lay bleeding and in the throes of a seizure in the back of that truck. She took it while James was plausibly dying of an overdose. And even after I told her what had happened, how scared I was for my brother, she didn't give it back. She *pretended* to look for it with me. She kept it purposefully hidden so that I'd have to focus on saving her brother instead of mine.

She lied.

I lost my virginity to her, got shot in the chest, witnessed Adam blowing his brains out, endured torture, and braved the darkness over and over again for her.

And she lied.

She has no idea how to stitch things together, only tear them apart.

I can't stay here ... can't wrap my mind around a betrayal like this.

"He's going. You've got all cameras recording?" Cory's talking to the ceiling again. His voice sounds like he's underwater.

I blip.

Chapter Twenty

It's dark. Not the darkness, just regular old nighttime dark, but all my time up-tree has wired me to fear it now. Carpet fibres mat under my bare feet, worn and grainy. My heartbeat thunders in my head as I grope through the darkness and then stumble when my hip cracks into a chair. Wincing, I find a wall and the pale outline of a door. "James?" I whisper, but there's no sound other than me in here. No breathing. Nothing.

I fumble for a switch and flick on the light to find that I'm in a cramped bedroom. Last time I was here, there were textbooks littering the desk, an unmade bed, and a trail of cough syrup bottles leading to my overdosing brother.

"James," I croak, fear solidifying in my chest, dense as setting concrete. I take in a single bed stripped down to its mattress. The desk is bare. So are the shelves. Vacuum lines zigzag the carpet and the air smells like bleach and Windex. He's not here. *No, no, no.* "James!"

I stumble toward the closet, crank open the door and find nothing but a rod and a row of wire hangers, Backing away from it, I gulp for air. He's not dead. He's not. He's all I have left. "James, hello?" I can't breathe. My legs feel soupy and when I look down, the floor is solid, it's not the darkness, it's me. Losing it. Losing my grip on everything. I'm cracking.

I slump onto the bare mattress as the first sob leaks out of me. God, I messed up. Charlie never felt for me like I did for her. Cory was never my friend. It was all an act I naively fell for. She sidelined me into helping Adam when I could have been here instead. The Embassy is wholesale murdering people, shipping off babies into far-branch worlds fully aware that those places will likely erase them. That's on me. All on me. That's what happens when I'm loud, when I stand out, I pay for it. Every single time.

Oh God, I can't lose her and Cory and then James too. I can't. And I can't stop the sobs as they twist out of me in this gutted room.

The door smashes open and I leap to my feet, expecting icy howls and claws and needle teeth. Expecting death.

"Freeze, motherfucker!" A thin guy in boxer shorts grips a baseball bat like he's ready to swing for the fence. "I'll knock your head off."

I hold out my trembling hands. My bandaged finger looks like a white sausage. Everett's tobacco tin has left chips of paint on my fingers. "Not armed. It's just a tin. I'm not armed." I mustn't look even remotely threatening because the bat sags as the guy squints at me. I can only imagine what he sees, a pale, barefoot ghost in a hospital gown, tears streaking down a hollow face.

"How the hell did you get in here?" He flexes his fingers on the bat. I recognize him. James's best friend. He practically lived at our house when the pair of them weren't playing Little League together. They're roommates now. His name bubbles up through the sludge of my mind.

"Micah," I gulp. "Y-you guys left the front door unlocked. I'm looking for James."

He leans away from me, rattled that I know him. Of course, he doesn't know me. Even if he pegged me as James's oddly quiet little brother, I haven't recognized my own reflection in the mirror these past few days, and I don't expect anyone else to.

"James is gone," he says. "Has been for weeks."

I claw through the panic rising in me and choke the question out,

"Gone home?" Please, please let it be that.

"His mom picked him up."

Relief hits me harder than Micah's bat would have. My guts drop and my vision swims. I press my tingling hands against my wet eyes. "Home?" My voice hops up an octave.

"Yes, home. Jesus, you alright? Do you need a ride somewhere?" Micah's voice is guarded as he raises the bat again, putting together the implications of what a flaked-out, rail-thin intruder wearing nothing but a hospital gown might mean.

The darkness shifts below me, like a sea monster showing its streamlined flank just below the water's surface. Screw that. I'm not going back yet. "I'm good. I'm just ... worried about him, you know? He was going to call me. Is he okay?"

"Will be, once he gets into rehab, I expect. How about I call you a cab? I'll pay. Take you wherever you need to go." He backs toward the door. "I'm just going to go get the phone, okay? Chill."

I nod. He's not calling a cab and we both bloody well know it. The carpet starts disintegrating under my feet. "Hey, can I use your bathroom?" I blurt. He can't see this next bit—me fighting off the darkness.

"Knock yourself out. It's at the end of the hall." Micah points with the bat and clears the doorway so I can get by.

"Thank you," I mumble, wrapping my arms around myself and shouldering past him.

The whole corridor wobbles like a suspension bridge and I lunge for the door at the end of it and skid into the bathroom, slamming the door behind me just as the white ceramic tiles on the floor start to crumple inward like broken teeth. One of them cuts into my ankle as my feet squeak and slide on the uneven surface. I clutch at the sink and grit my teeth. "No. I'm not leaving yet. I'm going to him."

But the darkness knows me down to my molecules. It knows I'm too tired to resist, too cracked to hold together right now. It knows I want James more than anything and it's gleefully plucking me away from him.

"Please." My fingers slip on the porcelain sink. "Please don't." I've never pled with it like this. My stomach drops as it burbles with elation at my weakness. And then it eats me slowly, like a dog savouring a soup bone. It gnaws at my shins, crushes my hips, drags my torso through broken tile, every shard scraping at my ribcage as it sucks me under in contracting waves, like birthing, but in reverse.

"You okay in there?" Micah bangs on the door.

No. Let me see him. Please. Please, I'll do anything. I grip the tobacco tin to my chest and whimper as I go under.

Cory bends over me, swearing and shaking my shoulder. IDOCS curl poised in front of my face like a cobra raised up to strike. I swat them away. I'm curled up on the cold acrylic floor. My hand is empty. I don't have the tin, I realize, blinking up at the big man in horror. He's holding it, slipping it into his chest pocket as he straightens. "No. Please." Not him too. I can't trust anyone. "Cory. I need to go back. Give it back, please."

I try to stand but collapse, so I pull myself toward him instead.

"Sorry, kid. I really am." He backs away, eyes heavy with pain. Behind him, through the plexiglass, four armed men stand with their guns pointing uncertainly at us. "Not my choice. Embassy says you get one trip a week, and you just took it. Next time, okay? Hang in there."

"My brother," I wail. The floor hums mechanically beneath me. Rage buzzes through my joints, drones like a hornet's nest in my chest. The door is opening, and Cory is backing toward it. "I need to see my brother!" I howl and crash toward him, but I'm too late.

The IDOCS on the floor trip me up. I slam onto my side, bruising my ribs and knocking the wind out of me. The hamster ball door rotates closed and the armed escort shuffles Cory out of the room while

I wheeze on the floor, rage and pain and raw terror flooding through me like ocean breakers, each one more powerful than the last.

When I can breathe again, I groan and drag myself toward the bathroom. I don't want them to see me like this. Pathetic, red-faced, crawling across the floor. I'm going and they can't stop me. I need to see if James is alright. As I'm pulling myself over the lip of stainless steel that delineates the bathroom cubicle from the rest of the circular cell, I drink in the adrenalin rising in me. The whole room pulses in time with my heart. I rake the accordion door closed and an announcement squeals over the intercom.

"Mr. Enril, you need to come out and calm down, or we'll drop the oxygen levels."

"Do it," I roar.

My limbs crackle with fire. They can go to hell, all of them. I'm going to James, and they can't stop me. Clutching my head in my hands, I breathe out through my mouth and picture my parent's bungalow, the rusted Ford Econoline out front, Dad's tired smile, Mom's frenetic movements, the shuddering bass of the twins playing videogames in the basement, James's firm handshake, his stubborn sense of pride. How they loved me. I wasn't even theirs and they loved me.

The air fizzes around me, raising hair on my arms. I drop through the rage, let my limbs go lax in the heat of it. My head falls back against the edge of the cold sink.

And then I go.

I don't need Everett's tin at all. I know my way to James.

So, I just go.

The grass is slippery and ice cold with dew. A full moon rakes shadows across the back lawn and turns the pear tree outside the kitchen window into a black spiderweb of bare branches. No lights stream from the kitchen save the blinking green digital clock on the microwave.

12:00. Power blip.

But there's a lamp on in James's bedroom. And the blinds are up.

Grass sticks to my feet and a stinging wind ripe with the crisp, syrupy scent of autumn presses the hospital gown against my legs. I shuffle toward the yellow rectangle of light the window throws into the back yard with my heart in my throat.

A dog bays down the block, restless in the confines of its back yard.

Dad hasn't mowed the lawn. The odd thought crops up as I edge forward through thick grass past my ankles. *Something's wrong.* He's a lawn worshipper, spends his spring, summer and fall weekends smelling of fertilizer, weed spray and clippings. He edges the grass on his hands and knees with a goddamned pair of scissors—I swear to God.

Now that I'm here, creeping through the back yard I grew up in, a deep fear roots around my heart. What if they're not okay? What if my leaving did something to my family, like Charlie did to Adam.

James was always a straight shooter. Drank a bit. Smoked the occasional cigarette, but he never got into anything hard, even when the twins were experimenting. He's the last person in the world I'd expect to overdose on opioids, but I'd seen it. Had *I caused* it? I shuffle to a stop in the slab of light. Do I even want to look in his window and see the waves I've left in my wake?

Everything else is a Goddamned mess, more tangled up than the dimensions I've hopped through these past weeks. Was I really arrogant enough to think I could save my family from something this malignant? That I was stronger than the darkness trying to get through our cottage door? It touched James just like it touched me, this cosmic predator that catalogues the taste of everything it's ever sampled. Did I think it would let my brother slip out of its grip once it grabbed his ankle?

Yeah.

That's exactly what I was hoping for. What I need to confirm.

That it's let go of him. That he has his life back.

I need for him to be okay. I need to see it.

His bedroom window is too high for me to peer into from the lawn, but the garden shed against the back fence is tall enough, and God knows we all scaled it enough times as kids, enough for me to memorize every anchor point on the way up to its slanted roof with the green curling shingles. We used to watch falling stars up there with Dad.

I pull back from the square of warm light and I climb up onto the shed.

There's a book open on a desk at the end of James's unmade bed. The chair is pushed back and unoccupied. I can't see him. I stand on my tiptoes and crane my neck, but I don't see shadows moving from elsewhere in the room.

Then, something moves out here. Like wind through the grass.

The darkness. It circles lazily, a shark in the deep, but its slow circuits aren't closing on the shed I stand on. Instead, it's lapping progressively closer to the house.

"No," I whimper as I realize what I've done.

It doesn't want me because it knows I'm a guaranteed meal and it's chewed me up enough times that I've lost my appeal. It wants something fresh and untainted. It wants James and I brought it right to him.

I'm the bait. I'm supposed to be the one keeping the darkness away, but it's tied to me, and I've towed it to the people I love most. The thought collapses like a black hole in my chest. My God, I am sick of being used, being manipulated, being alone. My emotions condense to a singularity, a massive gravity pulling at my bones, sinking through my organs.

You're not alone. You're tied to it, but it's tied to you too.

The backyard thrashes, like something caught in a net. Grass shivers, soil tears, and roots pop.

A small smile tugs at the corner of my mouth. *Don't let it ever touch James again. You are the Gulf. It can't cross to him without you, and it damn well knows it.* I drop my gaze from James's window.

Something screeches between my ears, like a mass of maneaters on the horizon of my mind.

The dog down the alley goes berserk.

I back away from my house, letting my feet shuffle to the far edge of the garden shed roof where it butts up against the fence and the back alley below. It's not a big drop, maybe nine feet to the pavement, but I'm pretty sure my skull will crack open if I hit it headfirst.

The darkness tugs at me, urging me back toward the house, thin ribbons of smoke nipping at my wrists and ankles.

"Fuck you," I whisper, and I spread my arms wide, and tip backward off the shed, like it's an Olympic diving platform and I'm going for gold. The darkness can either swallow me or let me die.

My stomach lurches at the freefall.

The hospital gown flutters against my thighs.

The world falls silent.

And as the alley warps and blackness envelops me in acrid, roiling anger, a deep conviction sinks its teeth into me. I'll never see James or the rest of my family again. I know something else too, by how forcefully the darkness crams down my nostrils, punches past my mouth and slashes at my insides. It's pissed. More than I've ever felt it. Because I dangled my family before it and then yanked them out of its reach again. Because I thwarted it, and something as trifling and small and pathetic as me shouldn't have been able to do that.

I smile again, baring my teeth as it chokes me.

Bring it on you son of a bitch. I've got nothing left to lose.

Epilogue

James

On the drive home from the cottage, after we remembered David, I made Dad stop at the Gulf station where I bought an insanely over-priced notebook and a pack of ballpoint pens. All the way home, heedless of the bumps, I furiously wrote down everything I could recall about my kid brother, consumed by the fear that this—this *remembering*—was something fragile and temporary, that the world would try to take him away from us again if given the chance. And I wasn't giving David back. No fucking way.

The initial writing looks like the hasty scribbles of a six-year-old, but I don't care. I keep the notebook by my bed, beside the John Grisham novel, and I add to it when I recall details. Dad and I have somewhat convinced Mom and the twins that what we experienced was real and we're not batshit crazy, and slowly, recollections are bubbling up in them too. We even huddle around the phone to make group calls to my older siblings, Julie, Justine and Jeremiah, probing none-too-subtly to see if they've been having nightmares, if they remember David. My eldest brother thinks the call is some sort of elaborate family prank, says the only David he knows is an asshole at work with a combover and a corvette.

The girls, however, are subdued and concerned when we call them. Both of them have separately booked time off work and are coming home to see us next week.

Since then, I've been studying thermal expansion coefficients, conductivity, and preheat temperatures. At first, I thought the broken skeleton key was brass or iron, but after performing spark tests on it, I've come to the baffling conclusion that it's composed of something else entirely, an alloy I've never seen.

And it's just what I need. A puzzle, something to hyperfocus on that gets me out of my slump and one step closer to finding David.

I look up every antique store and pawn shop in the area and buy them all out of skeleton keys. Then I pick the most likely matches, zip cut them in half and prep them for welding. My first five attempts at fusing a new handle onto the broken shaft result in thermal cracks or disappointingly brittle joints. So, I use buttering, welding a transition layer onto both base metals to reduce the risk of defects. It takes poring over several charts on welding dissimilar metals, and four more attempts after that to get it right, but this morning, I did it.

I'm holding it in my hand. A freshly buffed, whole skeleton key. No warping. No cracks.

This is what I'm built to do, join dissimilar things together until they stick, until they're whole. I've done it with my eccentric family members since I was a kid. Smiled like a champ when things were brittle, welded us all together even when we didn't want to hold. Damn if that's not a goldmine for some therapist down the road.

The key rests in my palm, unnaturally warm even though I've given it plenty of time to cool. There's gravity to it. It almost hums. I don't even wash up. Peeling off my welding leathers, I creep into the house, and snag the keys to Mom's car off the front entry table. I'm backing it out of the driveway before she even knows it's gone. She'll forgive me if I gas it up for her when I get back and buy that new set of front brakes and rotors the shop in town has quoted way too much to repair.

I head onto the highway with the freshly made key clattering in the central console cupholder.

Hope perches in my chest, higher and lighter than I remember feeling it for a long time. God, I've missed this, this rush of pushing above the mire and monotony of the everyday world to strive for something impossible. This is worlds away from sweating my bag off in a hospital with an infected foot and chronic nightmares.

Honey Bear Hollow cottage resort is a three-hour drive from our house, but the sky is light and cloudless, and I find an eighties station that's cranking out classics by The Ramones, Agent Orange, and the Dead Kennedys. The raw guitar, angry bass, and growling lyrics pound through me until I'm slapping the steering wheel and singing along. For the first time in a long time, I feel whole. Focused.

When I get there, I drive right past Angus's Quonset office and dodge the potholes all along Sweet Bee Circle. The lake is midnight blue with the first pristine layer of ice spanning its surface like polished marble, but it doesn't hold my attention. My chest tingles at the sight of a small yellow cottage at the end of the lane with a comfortably deep covered porch and charming six pane windows. I pull Mom's car into the driveway, grab the key, and take the porch steps two at a time as the cooling engine ticks and chickadees chatter in the trees behind the house.

This place. Even emptied out it holds all my best memories. Dad and I were just here, yet there's always this discordant feeling when I come back, like I've been gone for a lifetime and never left at the same time. Like there's two of me, one here where I belong, and one scrambling to find a place in school, at work, with friends.

The screen door doesn't squeak when I open it. Its hinges have been freshly oiled. Someone's repainted all the white trim this week. I can smell it and touch a finger to a window frame, but it's not tacky. The front door is locked. I expected that, but I didn't expect the hardware to be changed out for a new silver knob that doesn't fit the feel of the place at all. The renovations Angus spearheaded are sucking the warmth out of the old place. *My God, please tell me they didn't replace the interior knobs.* Cupping my hands, I peek in the front window and take in the bare, unfurnished interior, gaping and wide open like a gutted carcass.

"Hey." A deep, aggravated voice calls from far behind me. I turn to see Angus Tyler, the proud proprietor of Honey Bear Hollow, waddling up the gravel road toward me. "You can't just drive on in here. The sign says stop at the office!"

I flash him a grin and wave like I can't hear him. Then I pull my jacket sleeve over my fist and bust the pane of glass in the front door.

"Hey! Stop," Angus barks. He comes to a shocked stop halfway between the cottage and his office. "I'm calling the police. You hear?"

I ignore him, reach through the shattered glass, and twist the deadbolt free.

"You little sonofabitch." He cranks his hat down tighter as I wave at him again. "I've got a 7mm rifle at the shop. I'm going to get it right now and you have exactly one minute to get your punk ass off my property before I use it."

One minute is more than I need.

I open the front door and duck inside.

It's cold. I catch a whiff of fresh cut lumber and chalky drywall, new scents foreign to a place that's meant to smell like furniture polish, woodstove smoke and mothballs. Like all my childhood summers.

The closet door that used to lead to the new addition is gone. The whole original wall's been knocked down and an ugly support column propped up in its place. That's okay. I don't think I need the closet door. When I found Dad here last week, looking lost and clutching a piece of David's childhood art, when it all flooded back to us who we'd been missing, we sat on the floor together for awhile. I'd noted then that the renovators had left the original bedroom doors up. They'd slapped on a patchy coat of ugly grey paint, but left the original hardware intact, crystal doorknobs and skeleton key locks.

They're still here, thank Christ.

As Angus Tyler quick walks up the road away from me, I cross the living room in four strides. Everything echoes in the empty space. My boots on the hardwood, my breath too fast and too loud. I stop in front of the bunkroom I used to sleep in as a kid.

The door is open, and the bunks have all been torn out. Goddamnit, why does that hurt so much? I haven't slept in there since I was small. I grab the cool crystal knob in my hand and slowly close the door until its latch clicks.

Fishing into my pocket, I pull out the skeleton key. It feels dense as lead. The teeth slide into place into the keyhole. A jolt goes up my wrist as I twist the handle and the lock snicks closed. Taking a deep breath, I turn it back.

Unlock the door.

Open it.

"Jesus fucking Christ," the words slip past my lips.

The empty bedroom is gone. A reflection of the cottage kitchen as I remember it stands in its place. The old Philco fridge. The lace curtains on the window. It's storming outside.

Spine tingling, I jiggle the key out of its lock, close the door behind me, and step into a strange mirror world.

Hang tight, brother. I'm coming.

ACKNOWLEDGEMENTS

Thanks always to my best friend and husband Colin for supporting me, loving me, and bringing me endless snacks and ice-cold pops. What more could a writer need? Liam and Finn, any sweetness, kindness, and humour I inject into my characters comes from you. Al Hess, Darby Harn, Jennifer Lane, and Megan King thank you for taking the time to bravely wade through the early drafts of Breach. Because of your incredible talent, graceful feedback, and unswerving support as critique partners and good friends, this book is worlds better than what I would have crafted if left to my own devices. Michelle McLachlin, thank you for believing in my writing and championing my work, and Shona Kinsella, thank you for polishing it. It takes a small army to get a book out into the world, and my small army is the best. Thank you all.

ABOUT THE AUTHOR

At a young age, SHELLY CAMPBELL wanted to be an air show pilot or a pirate, possibly a dragon and definitely a writer and artist. She's piloted a Cessna 172 through spins and stalls, and sailed up the east coast on a tall ship barque—mostly without projectile vomiting. In the end, Shelly found writing and drawing dragons to be so much easier on the stomach. Shelly writes speculative fiction ranging from grimdark fantasy, to sci-fi and horror. She'd love to hear from you.

www.shellycampbellauthorandart.com
https://twitter.com/ShellyCFineArt
https://www.instagram.com/shellycampbellfineart
https://www.facebook.com/shellycampbellauthorandart
https://www.tiktok.com/@shellycampbellauthor?

More from Eerie River

Eerie River Publishing is a leader in independent horror, dark fantasy, and dark speculative fiction.

We are dedicated to publishing anthologies, collections, and novels from some of the best indie authors around the world. Our goal is to become a go-to resource for horror, dark fantasy and dark speculative readers, and to provide a safe space for authors to share their stories.

Interested in becoming a Patreon member?
By joining our patreon, you will be supporting our artists and authors, who work hard to produce high-quality and original content for your enjoyment. You will also get access to exclusive perks, such as early releases, behind-the-scenes updates, bonus material, and more. If you love dark fiction and want to support independent publishing, please consider becoming a patron today. Thank you for your interest and support.

www.patreon.com/EerieRiverPub

To stay up to date with all our new releases and upcoming giveaways, follow us on Facebook, Twitter, Instagram and YouTube.

linktr.ee/eerieriver

EERIE RIVER PUBLISHING

NOVELS & COLLECTIONS
Gulf: Dark Walker Series Book One (2023)
Breach: Dark Walker Series Book Two (2024)
Chasing The Dragon: Horror Vigilante Novel (2023)
The Naughty Corner: Novella Collection (2023)
Dead Man Walking: Nick Holleran Series (2022)
Devil Walks in Blood: Nick Holleran Series (2022)
The Darkness In The Pines: Nick Holleran Series (2023)
At Eternity's Gate: Empire of Ruin Series (2023)
Beyond Sundered Seas: Empire of Ruin Series (2023)
Path of War: Empire of Ruin Series (2022)
In Solitudes Shadow: Empire of Ruin Series (2022)
The Void: Sapphic Fiction (2023)
They Are Cursed Like You: Trailer Park Witches Series (2023)
Infested: Horror Novel (2022)
SENTINEL: The Bensalem Files (2021)
NOTHUS: The Bensalem Files (2022)
Miracle Growth: A Cosmic Horror Novella(2022)
Helluland: Urban Fantasy of Legends (2023)
A Sword Named Sorrow: Fantasy Novel (2022)
Storming Area 51 (2019)

ANTHOLOGIES
Year of the Tarot: Four Book Series
AFTER: A Post-Apocalyptic Survivor Series
Elemental Cycle: Four Book Series
It Calls From Series
Blood Sins
Last Stop: Whiskey Pete
Of Fire and Stars
From Beyond the Threshold

DRABBLE COLLECTIONS
Forgotten Ones: Drabbles of Myth and Legend
Dark Magic: Drabbles of Magic and Lore

COMING SOON
Hell Over Haven: Nick Holleran book by David Green
The Roots Run Deep: Collection of Horror by C.M. Forest
Rotten House: Horror Novel by by Michelle River
The Earth Bleeds at Night: Anthology of Horror

New Remastered Cover and Interior!
Gulf: Dark Walker Series Book One

Out Now! By Award Winning Author C.M. Forest
The Roots Run Deep

Award Winning Novel by C.M. Forest
Infested

"The Craft" meets "My Best Friends Exorcism"
They Are Cursed Like You

Cosmic Horror Novella
Miracle Growth

9 781998 112340